THE 23RD GIRL

I0623477

HALF BAKED BEANS

PUBLISHING

THE 23RD GIRL

Written by
DIVYA RATAN
ROHAN KACHALIA

Story Concept by

CHETAN SONI

HALF BAKED BEANS LITERATURE

e-mail: publish.halfbakedbeans@gmail.com

First Published by Half Baked Beans in 2017

Acknowledgement

I'm grateful to Half Baked Beans for giving me the opportunity to finish what Rohan started. It was pure serendipity. My project as a co-author began after being selected in the short story writing competition the publishers ran on their Facebook page early last year. As I was writing a novel for the first time, I did hit a few bumps along the way initially. I have to thank the team of Half Baked Beans for having been a constant support system for everything and making my maiden attempt a very smooth process.

A word of thanks goes to Gaurav Tiwari, my dear husband for having relentlessly pushed me back into writing when a long hiatus dulled the shine off my written expression. It was tough but it got easier as it's always nice to have someone believe in you so much and always have your back. He also patiently listened to me and gave me his feedback on how the story was going along. Not to forget he was the one I turned in to first for editing the script after I had nit-picked it for errors before submitting it to Half Baked Beans for feedback. So he has actually been through a lot, I should say!

I would also like to thank my friend Siddhesh Kabe for helping me out with tips on how not to start a novel, how to develop characters and various other inputs during the course of writing the script. We were in touch when I was editing his science fiction novel - Ragnarok: The fate of Gods, published by Half Baked Beans last year. It is an epic tale about 'the deep and secretive world of fringe science'.

My co-author Rohan Kachalia was very patient and confident of my skills. I am sure he would have had a few reservations when I scrapped entire chapters and rewrote them but the entire process has been a very amicable and synergistic one. We rarely ever disagreed on how the story was shaping up in my hands. Most importantly, I have to thank Chetan Soni from Half Baked Beans for his continuous support and follow-up which helped keep things on proper track.

And finally, thanks to you, dear reader for picking this book up. I hope you like it as much as we loved writing it!

-   Divya Ratan

I would like to thank my publisher for having faith in my writing and being patient with me.

I would like to express my gratitude to my wife, Hetal, who supported and encouraged me to write.

My parents for being there for me and understanding my inclination towards writing.

My friends for their constant appreciation and feedbacks.

Last but not the least, to my readers. Thank you for picking the book and hope you enjoy reading.

-   Rohan Kachalia

CHAPTER 1

BANGGG!!!

Was it a meteor? An Air Strike? An Earthquake? Or did the Sun blast off surges of intolerable levels of heat and energy into the atmosphere?

Turned out, it was none of the above. It was just Rashv falling flat on his well-rounded stomach causing a mild tremor of 2.3 on the Richter scale. And no, the earth beneath didn't tremble as it usually does during an earthquake but something else did tremble - the insides of his stomach; so much so that it caused his stomach to rumble with a loud gurgling noise ending with a loud BURRRP!

"Ouch, this hurts!" Rashv coughed as he checked his forehead. He sensed that a slight bump had come up on his forehead as a result of the fall. It felt a bit hot. "Aargghh... I have been daydreaming again!" sighed the poor guy. Judging from his injuries, one could say that it must hurt pretty badly when you fall from the material height of about 2 feet and that too in a semi-conscious state. It hurts even more when you realise that all the mushy feelings you had been rolling in were only from a dream.

Before we find out what happens next, let us take a moment to introduce you to Rashv Patel. Whether or not he emerges to be the hero of this story is reserved for another time! For now, let us know that Rashv was an ordinary guy leading an ordinary life. Sixteen? Twenty? Twenty-five? His burly frame defied his innocent looking face and made it extremely tough for anyone to draw any assumptions about his age. Perhaps it had something to do with his height of 5 feet 4 inches matched with a weight which was a tad more than what could be considered as socially acceptable. Or the fact that he had a very sweet dimple on his right cheek which was now reduced to a pinpoint with all the rosy flesh on his soft cheeks. He was the plump child who became a plump youth... just the kind of easygoing, happy-go-lucky kid who one never thinks can have any issues with Life; for if ever you were to meet him, you would be struck with his ringing laughter and the innocence of his round face shaped by a thick head of dark black hair. His black eyes sparkled and shone with hope and warmth but if you cared to know him a bit deeper than you met him on the surface, you would most certainly detect a bit of anger or boredom, the dangerous moods that almost always meant that there was some pain lurking in the dark corners of the soul.

At college, Rashv was a geek. Mr. Know-it-all. The kind of guy you would rather spot in the library than anywhere else. He was the one with all the answers but the only thing he struggled with was his own self-confidence. And of course, being a bit on the heavier side is never easy for a young heart.

Let us now come back to the present moment and what it holds. Rashv closed his eyes and took in the surroundings with a deep breath as he lay on the floor - the soft breeze blowing in, the curtains flapping, the persistent tick-tock of the clock, the whirring sound produced by the incessant rotations of the fan, the street dogs barking, and an occasional honking of a car passing by; all just to be doubly sure that he was in his senses and still very much alive.

It was about 5 a.m. Life had begun to trickle out on the streets down below.

"How beautiful mornings are, indeed", he observed and sighed.

An unexpected roll-out of your bed sometimes makes you witness nature's bountiful beauty. Perhaps it looks as breathtaking because it is more or less unexpected that the trade-off for a tragically shortened sleep can be such a beautiful sight for one's half-opened eyes.

A cool breeze carrying the scents and sounds of a new

morning tingled his senses alive. A beautiful cloud, kissed pink by the early morning sun flitted slowly through the sky as if in a dream. The faraway horizon was dipped in shades of crimson shyness till stroke by stroke of golden light, the sky was slowly covered in the radiance of a new day.

"Ahh! Bliss!" Rashv smiled as the heat of the first rays of the morning hit his skin and started warming half of the face of the Earth.

"God, when will I be the Rashv that my semi-conscious state dreams of, wildly popular and with no cares whatsoever in this whole wide world?" he sighed.

"Rashv, stop whining about the absence of a pretty damsel in your life and forget it. There's much more to Life than that." He surprised himself with this sudden self-correcting soliloquy.

"Whoever you are, whatever you do, your life wouldn't matter as much to anyone else. Whether you are rich or poor, whether you possess the entire world's happiness or are sunk deep into sorrows, it is only you who are in control of your life. So stop complaining and start enjoying Life by actually living it up." He smiled as he was inadvertently reminded of his mom's most repeated words. Mom's favourite advice had started playing at the back of his mind by itself. He chuckled.

Rashv's mom, like most Indian mothers, represented the single most important influence in his life. She was a soft woman of a smallish frame with an olive brown skin which accentuated the warmth of her personality. Age had added laugh lines around her smiling mouth and crow's feet around her gleaming eyes, indicating the fullness with which she had lived her life. In fact, everything about her was so gentle and bright that life somehow seemed less of a bother with her around. She was Rashv's constant pillar of strength and motivation. She had twice the amount of a loving heart full of care, love and devotion for her only son. At times, Rashv would even pretend to look for the invisible cape his supermom hid from him as she raised him perfectly, singlehandedly! Sometimes in the thick of a sleepless night, he wished that his constantly travelling executive dad could be there for him too. But then he still had no regrets as he had the most loving set of parents, maybe, in the whole wide world.

Rashv caught the flapping curtain and squeezed the cloth into his palm, as he took its support to lift his weight up. It felt like it took him ages to stand up on his feet. But on the contrary, it didn't take even a minute for the curtain rod to give up on him and land on the floor with a loud lingering metallic sound threatening to wake up the entire neighborhood.

"You cannot trust anything these days. Screw you!" Rashv lamented and stormed off for a hot shower. He splashed some cold water onto his face and checked the bump in the bathroom mirror. He stood close; eyes wide open, diagnosing the bump which had turned slightly red by now. "Aargh", he retorted, softly caressing the bump. It took a few moments for the water to turn hot and judging the time perfectly, Rashv stood right under the shower head, taking the water directly on his face. The hot water shower kind of worked as a mini massage for him and relieved him of stress and tension by soothing the stiff muscles of his neck, shoulders, and back. He felt as alive and rejuvenated as a fish when it's put back into the water after being taken out of it. As he put on a comfortable sleeveless tee and his favourite striped Tommy Hilfiger boxers, he noticed that he seemed to look a tad taller than his small frame.

"Did I lose some weight here? Hmm... Not bad!" he said, turning to the side in front of the full-length mirror and screening himself, head to toe.

The slight excitement on his face died a quick death as soon as his gaze fell on the red bump on his forehead. He pulled a face fearing a panic attack from his mom… "What, why, when, where, how…" Rashv prepared himself with an acceptable excuse in response to the endless queries his mom would surely put him through in some time. And then suddenly he noticed his phone. 5 missed calls! It was Rahul, his best friend from college. He was reminded that his best buddy had asked him to come up to his apartment last evening to discuss and help arrange their outfit for the Annual Traditional Day at college scheduled for the next day. He decided to look for his mom and catch up with Rahul who stayed in the same building.

"What a mess!" Rashv's expression changed once again; from a frown to that of utter dismay upon seeing the broken curtain rod. He kicked the rod hard as he crossed the room to reach his cupboard and in the rage of the moment stubbed his toe instead.

"Ughh… Not again!" He screeched to no one in particular and limped his way to the kitchen to look for his mom. That's the thing with Indian parents. You may have grown up to any age, but you need to always keep them informed about your whereabouts. Not finding his mom anywhere close and deciding to keep up the deal he had made with his parents regarding the 'informing' part, Rashv left a note on the fridge. "I am going over to Rahul's place. I'll be back in an hour. Love, RV"

Rashv had since forever quarreled with his parents for changing his name to something simpler and easier to pronounce. When he was just four and his parents had to pick up a name for the school, Rashv's dad was quite insistent on choosing a rare, stand-out name for his child. But in that age when children can barely make themselves understood in their broken mother tongue, all Rashv could respond to the query of "what's your name?" was with a hiss.. Raasss…vv. He used to say, bending his head forward and trying hard to get his name out of his mouth. He looked quite adorable doing

5

that and he realised it soon enough as every response to that question got him a pinch on both cheeks and maybe a lipstick mark or two on them thereafter. He got so fed up of this that he decided that his name must surely have something evil about it and he stopped responding to shady aunties since he thought that he had nothing to do with them. As he grew up he had to frequently deal with other people mispronouncing his hard name. As such, in desperation, he shortened it to RV and had his friends call him by it. He decided that RV meant Random Variable and he could take on any value that he liked… meaning he could choose what he wanted to do. Labeling that as cool enough, he left it at that, thereby solving the problem and a lot of heartburn for himself.

Rashv limped out of his room to get into the lift. It was still some time before the daily madness began and they had about two hours before the first class was scheduled to begin.

"Stop! Stop! Stop! Wait for me!" he waved at the people in the lift as he just managed to stop the lift doors from closing and literally squeezed himself through the doors and in between the people in the lift. Time and lifts wait for none. It seemed that they all shared this piece of knowledge which prevented them from waiting for the other lift to descend and board this one instead.

Rashv was made uncomfortable by the screening eyes of people as he entered the lift. It was strange. Sometimes he simply could not understand as to why people stared at him right down to the foot, as if taking mental note of his dress and shoes. Two women next to him were deep in hushed conversation, unfazed by the disturbance caused by Rashv's forced entry into the cramped space. They suddenly burst into laughter and buoyed by their light mood, their hair strands caused quite a turbulence in the delicate linings of his nose.

"Achhooo!!!"

Rashv rubbed his twitching nose and wondered whether their

sudden burst of happiness had got anything to do with him. He strained to get a tab on the topic of their conversation but the motley bunch of people packed inside the elevator made it a bit difficult for him to concentrate... like the kid with the gas balloons in his right hand who kept on stepping on his toe whenever the lift halted on a floor, with the balloons getting into his face; the businessman guy who turned back and gave Rashv a tough look whenever he received a jab in his ribs, the girl with a strange-looking pup in her hands which for some reason could not stop barking for any apparent reason at all... and so forth. Besides, it was quite stuffy inside and somebody smelt way too pleasant for everybody's comfort.

Thankfully the lift was emptied of half its crowd on the next floor. Rashv alighted and made his way across the lobby hall and over to Rahul's "organized" apartment where there were a time and space for everything under the ceiling so to say and at present, it seemed like it was a bad time to visit as it was the time for sprouts and juice as per Rahul's mom.

"Yikes... I should have called him to check what he was up to before coming up uninvited" Rashv made an impassioned plea not to be served the 'healthy breakfast' and managed to convince Rahul's mom that the real reason he couldn't join them was that he had already had his breakfast even though his insides were rumbling with hunger. They moved to Rahul's room to discuss about what all they could do for the Annual Traditional day, provided Rahul could stop drooling over the girl next door and her long, straight hair and about the fact that he had just managed to get her number when he went to pick up the newspaper that morning and met her across the hallway.

"Lucky dog! Let's get back to business now" Rashv barked as they both howled in synchronous laughter.

CHAPTER 2

"Fuchchas come in a line!"

It was the Annual Traditional Day at college. Everyone was dressed in their best traditional attires. The event was coordinated and hosted by the senior batches of the college and as such, interjections from them could not be avoided. At the start of the event, the freshers were expected to introduce themselves to the other students. Later, it was a day long schedule of other cultural events, music and dance followed by a small lawn party. Swarms of students dressed in their best could be seen making a beehive to the most awaited fun event of the year.

And then, suddenly they spotted the showstopper of the last year's event and the girls went berserk to just get a glimpse of the hottest guy in the college. It was Ayaan, who looked stunningly hot in his ethnic look with gelled hair, clean shave and a perfectly toned body. As he was used to such attention, his 'don't care' attitude made him look all the more irresistible to the girl clan.

"Do girls even know they look so silly sometimes." Rashv was irritated by the presence of a popular guy around them. He and his friends were standing in a group waiting for the event to start.

"Hi, Guys! How are you all?" a small voice diverted their attention.

They turned around to meet one of the most stunning sightings of the day.

"Heta!" they all exclaimed with open mouths, eyes as if popping out of their sockets.

Heta was their classmate. Timid was her middle name. She had no time for fashion trends and simplicity was her call no matter what the occasion was. She was known as one of the most studious pupils of the class, always perched on the first bench of the middle row with no one to accompany her and in her simplicity and hard work, she was the striking example of a sincere student. Or so it seemed till now as today she was the most beautiful sight to behold. She was dressed in a burgundy tank top and a black skirt with her open hair falling in soft twirls around her face and shoulders. Her pink cheeks matched the allure of her glossed lips and somehow it was difficult for Rashv to take his eyes off her. They had never thought that she could look so attractive - the quiet little girl who seemed to have nothing else to do other than indulge in books and theories. It was indeed the most pleasant surprise of the day. But it was also a matter of shock as the dress was clearly ill-suited to the occasion.

"What!! Did you know it's the Traditional Day today?" Rashv exclaimed.

"Yeah, I know that it is the college's Annual Traditional Day", she gave him an enigmatic smile that melted Rashv's heart into a chocolate puddle.

"But dear, one should never break the protocols! Wait till one of the seniors spot you!", he chuckled.

"Shut up and let us go inside", she took his arm and dragged him into the auditorium.

The event started with laughter and cheers as the most jovial of seniors took to the stage and the first round of introductions started. Rashv was known as the kid who got into the college with maximum marks and so he was the first to be called onto the stage with a lot of cheers from his friends and classmates. As he was from Surat, he was wearing an adorable frock dress and turban and looked cute as he introduced himself and his culture with a loud "Kemcho!" and was met with a huge round of applause.

"Hi! I am Rashv. An 18 years old Gujarati from the land of

happiness and prosperity", Rashv expressed an immaculate pride in his hometown and local culture. "Coming to my name, I know that it's a bit difficult for you to pronounce but I am sure when you get to know me, you would willingly get over any such hurdles", he chuckled to a crowd that was now roaring with laughter. "Just like my name which means the symbol of Love, I am here to spread love and happiness among everyone." He bowed and signed off to a huge round of applause.

One by one Rashv's friends came up on the stage and introduced themselves. Then it was time for something they all had been waiting for. It was Heta's turn to come up on the stage and explain her erratic choice. She was met with a gasp from the crowd as she walked up. It caused the presenter to chortle out the gum he had been chewing on.

She took on the mic and started to speak, "Hi! I'm Heta. You all know me as the girl who wears the same kind of clothes every day to college, or probably as someone who needs to 'get a life'. Yes, I am your very own never-approachable-the-first-bencher-and-ever-studious, Heta." She continued, "And the fact of the matter is I did get my life today, eighteen years back, on this very date. Yeah, it's my birthday today. I do know that it was not appropriate to wear a western outfit here and definitely not to wear a figure hugging one piece that accentuates my curves and presents me as a cosmopolitan woman rather than the boring girl I am known as. But I want to say that until today, I was seen in the kind of clothes that I felt comfortable wearing and went unnoticed by the entire college. But just as I wore this ultra modern, figure-enhancing dress, all necks turned, eyes rolled, a few from the male clan swooned! Not to say that I have been comfortable with all this sudden adulation and so much of it as I have never worn this kind of outfit before. But without meaning any disrespect to the protocol, I stand here, in front of you, more traditional at heart than meets the eye." Heta had almost poured her heart out letting out all the pent up frustration of being ignored and having no friends to talk to, leaving the entire audience shell-shocked to witness something like this. They were probably mesmerized by the sudden impromptu spiel that came as a tornado sweeping the broad daylights out of everyone. A few of the other girls even considered it to be a tactic to vie for male attention and come off as coquettish.

She smiled and bowed to a round of whistles and applaud that celebrated her new found confidence.

"See, I am the new popular girl in college", she declared to Rashv and friends as she pretended to pat her own back.

"First of all, a very happy birthday, you little devil! Far from inviting the ire of seniors and the dean, you were actually so cool up there", Rashv smiled.

The crowd booed and cheered as one after the other the introductions got over followed by an announcement for two of the coolest freshers to come up back on the stage for an impromptu act. As Rashv struggled with ideas, Heta quickly pulled out an artificial flower from her hair for him and crooned:

You'll sit all alone if you wait for the right time,

What are you hoping for, I'm here, and I'm ready,

Holding on tight, don't give away the end.

The one thing that stays mine,

Amazing still it seems, I'll be 23,

I won't always love what I'll never have...

In the moments that she was singing she was a luminous sight to behold. Rashv was besotted along with half of the other boys of the college. And, that little crimson flower in his hand was the color of a budding Love in Rashv's silent heart.

CHAPTER 3

"What mess have you made all over the house, Rashv?" burst out a visibly agitated Mom, pushing the bedroom door. "It's frightening to wake up one morning and discover that while you were asleep, your son went bonkers creating a total mess in the house", his mom continued her monologue in top pitch.

Rashv, who was not sleepy anymore, mainly due to the loud and angry tone of his mother, let out a wry smile as he yawned and stretched his arms wide taking in the morning sunrise as she stood right there, in front of him, waiting for an explanation for all the mess he had created.

"Relax Mom! It's the weekend."

"Good to see you alive, son. It is for the third time this week that you have slept for straight 24 hours and that too without prior intimation", hissed his infuriated mom.

"Mom, please! I am an adult now and have all the rights in the world to make my own decisions. And I can't inform you before I get so sleepy. And moreover I am under no obligation to be the same person as I was before or for that matter even a day ago", he ranted.

"And 23 missed calls mom? Seriously? What did you think? That I've lost it completely?" Rashv groaned looking at his smartphone. "I don't even have the freedom to enjoy a nice long sleep during vacations?" He pulled a bad face while turning away for a shower.

"Apparently son, you missed your mom's birthday", quipped his disappointed mother. Rashv literally stood his ground for a moment, realizing the real reason behind his mom's anger and to make up for it he hugged his mom tightly from behind, kissed her cheek and wished her with a wide smile on his face. "Sorry and Belated Happy Birthday, my dearest, sweetest, loveliest, Mom!"

"Thank you, Beta!" she exclaimed and gave Rashv a warm hug with faint tears of happiness glistening in her eyes. She ruffled his hair and asked him to get ready on time for lunch.

After a scrumptious lunch, which lasted for almost an hour, the duo celebrated the birthday over gossip and pastries that Rashv had ordered from the local cake shop. Their endless talk revolved around movies, places to visit and their future. They devoured the pastries till the very last piece of cake was visible on the dish. They were involved in their discussions when suddenly Rashv's phone buzzed. It was Rahul, his friend from college and coaching classes.

"What happened? Who was it?" asked his mom as she noticed a frown on Rashv's face.

"It was Rahul. The coaching classes I had decided to join have been preponed by a week and will commence from the coming Monday. I am yet to clean my entire room which is all messed up with DVDs, gaming consoles, books and fashion magazines. It's going to be tough! Why do we have to study so much!" There was a slight tone of disappointment in Rashv's voice.

"I've made up my mind. I want to be a parliamentarian", he suddenly announced to his mom who was caught a bit off guard by this sudden declaration.

"Aah... I got that. Less work and more fun, right?"

Rashv nodded his head with a childlike glee on his face.

CHAPTER 4

"Move to room number 5, 3rd floor for the next lecture", the professor announced to a cacophonous group of students.

The rollercoaster of academic life had already begun at college and Rashv got totally sucked into it. Life had become all about lectures, extra classes, coaching classes and then there was Heta - his beloved Heta. He sensed that something really had changed on the Traditional Day at college. She was definitely a lot more than the girl they had always known, he realised. The girl who sat without company on the front benches of the class had suddenly started to gain his attention. He found himself looking out for her in the class, smiling whenever he thought of her; his rotund cheeks turning plush with admiration every single time.

"Sorry, I'm late. May I come in sir?" asked a small voice stuck somewhere between fear and confidence.

Rashv's reverie of Heta was broken by her honey-dipped voice and he blushed. She came right in and sat beside her new-found friend.

"Hi, Rashv! How late am I?" she whispered to him, careful enough to not catch the attention of the professor.

"Not too late. Just by a few beats of my heart" Rashv thought to himself and smiled. "You are not late. The lecture had just started." Rashv was all zing and tingle for the remaining lecture. Like everytime she looked at him, he felt like he had touched a live wire. She was charming and he felt fat but one could not be expected to think straight when they are that close to being electrocuted.

Rashv had entered college with the best grades. He had been a throughout topper and an academic success at school. Although his grades were never the top of the pile, but he always managed to easily get the 2nd or 3rd rank. School life had always been all about focus and never in his life had he felt anything as emotionally intense as he was now feeling for Heta. Except for once in mid-school when he had scampered up enough courage to finally approach a girl he liked. He remembered that he had written one long mail pouring out his feelings for her, honestly and completely and he shuddered to hit the Send button on his desktop. But then he had to. There was no way he would have walked up to her and expressed his love. That was young love. The love of a shy kid, slightly on the heavier side, which was crushed with as much conviction as could be. She laughed at him. She shared it with her girls. He was made to feel like he was not good enough, not deserving of her attention. Rashv's self-confidence had come crashing down as he picked up the pieces of his tattered feelings and confidence and vowed to keep his broken heart closeted inside forever. They had been friends but not anymore. Rashv relegated all the friendship gifts exchanged with her to the back of his bookshelf and her memories to the back of his mind.

For indeed:

"There's a reason why we have ribcages.

Our hearts have wings."

And he kept that new knowledge on the forefront of his feelings. That year he lost his grades and he decided to never put his heart on the line for insensitive girls.

"Rashv Patel, please come and draw $5x+3y = 0$ on the board."

Ugh. He had missed the whole lecture! The professor had caught him distracted.

"My classes are not meant for smiling daydreamers!" He reprimanded.

Thankfully the bell rang signaling the end of the torture for everyone and a wake-up call for those who had been drugged into a deep slumber by the monotonous and boring class on Linear Equations.

"Heta, would you leave me your contact number?" Rashv asked her after the class.

"I don't yet carry a cell phone, Rashv. You can have my landline, its xx-xxxxx23" she replied as she collected her books and left.

Business Mathematics was a common class for Rashv and Heta. He had a lighter day after the class with friends and Heta went back to attend the other classes. But it seemed like she had pulled along his mind with her as every conversation he had for the rest of the day was repeatedly brought back to his new admiration.

"Knock, knock!

Mind calling Heart, mind calling Heart"

"What?" asked the Heart (After pondering for over a minute whether to reply or ignore the mind).

"Isn't it wise to leave such unfathomable things pertaining to girls, friends and love to The Almighty?"

"I don't know! The almighty has got better things to do I guess. I fear one day I will be left only with my own eternal self-love and attention, but for now, all of this makes perfect sense", chuckled the Heart.

Rashv's mind and heart were being pulled in different directions. He decided to meet Heta after the classes. He finally found her in the library going through the cards looking for reference books.

"Hi!"

"Hi! Help me with this Rashv. I can't seem to find these goddamned books."

They scraped through the library for the reference books

16

required for the class assignment. It was a long, patient search. Heta was not the talkative kind and the silence between them had become just too overbearing for Rashv, more so because all he wanted to do right now was to see her beautiful lips curl into words as she spoke, the flutter of her long eyelashes and the wave of her hands and long tapering fingers as she expressed herself in her own unique animated way. He came up with endless gossips and funny episodes from the lectures just to keep her constant attention. They sat down at the library table and began to take down notes from the books.

"Isn't this topic so boring?" Heta complained.

"Of course, it is! But nothing is boring when you have a good company", he suggested.

"Stop flirting!" she quipped.

"Knock! Knock! Mind calling Heart... Mind calling Heart..."

"Just say it Rashv! It will not get straighter than this" Rashv's heart was jumping in excitement.

"Wait... what if she says no? It's better to test waters first." The mind said.

"People who cannot decide are doomed by fate to stay single forever", the heart was trying to really egg him on. "It's now or never... Go for it Rashv!"

Rashv was shaken from his indecisiveness by this sudden thought. He somehow recollected his thoughts as he tried to steer the conversation in the direction his heart wanted.

"I mean it Heta, in every sense of the word. Don't you consider yourself a 'good company?" he winked.

"I do Rashv, but certainly not in the way you intend", she was quick in gauging his mind.

After silently looking at her for a couple of minutes, Rashv did manage to shore up enough courage to say what was really for him a small but a rather big sentence. "Heta... I... like you", he uttered... carefully, looking into her limpid eyes.

"... And I like you too, a lot!" She smiled back. "But let's keep it at that!" she sighed as she squeezed his right hand and began to collect her books. "Let's leave now and try to not miss the next lecture", she declared and stood up to leave.

Rashv ached as he felt his heart slip into his toes, quietly without a noise and just as disastrously. Why had he even tried!

CHAPTER 5

Darkness... When everything that you love has been taken from you so unexpectedly and suddenly, all you can feel is anger, loss and revenge. And darkness is not just a lack of light. At times, it is also a profound lack of spirit as any dejected spirit will tell you.

It was after several years that Rashv had allowed his self-confidence to take such a nosedive. He hit a familiar rock bottom once again when Heta politely refused his interest in him. All he could reason out of this situation was that he was physically unattractive and stout and maybe that's why she said all that she did.

Rashv decided to surrender himself to the hollowness he felt as he sunk into the bed with an anticipation to be able to have a restful sleep and to be able to forget his meaningless aspirations and more specifically the hopeless one he had just had. His dark room was an easy company to his wounded self.

Upon seeing her beloved son crawl directly into the bed after coming from college without any usual demands for Pasta or soup made Rashv's mother smell a rat.

"Don't ask me, ask Heta." He stated plainly to his rather befuddled mother as she stood there with a shake of her head expressing her disappointment and was about to say something when Rashv stopped her midway.

"Mom, please, gimme a break from your motivational exercise! The overdose is such that if I hear it just one more time, I swear I'll stop studying and try a hand at being a 'Life Coach' and spend the rest of my days at maybe one of those red-light areas giving free lectures on the same", snorted a fuming Rashv. His irritation was pretty evident. The sequence of events in the day had simply frustrated him. At this point of time, he just wanted to be left alone.

Not having anything to do and sleep deluding him, Rashv took to the internet on his smartphone. Twitter was his new-found addiction over which he discovered that people followed unknown people, tweeted and re-tweeted meaningless stuff. He plugged in his earphones with MJ's music threatening to quite blast his ear drums, as he silently lip-synced the lyrics while surfing the internet.

Plainly out of the blue, Rashv decided to go against his usual habit of reading the tweets on his timeline by re-tweeting 'Sometimes raising one's voice works. And when it matches your facial expressions, it's kind of an icing on the cake.', but all he got in return was an increase in followers from spam accounts. His heart sank and he googled 'Interesting tweets that get replies' without any luck as the results threw nothing concrete. Just as he was about to sign out from twitter, the notification tab read as "one", he clicked on it and it read:

"A rising as hard as steel that can lead one to the finish line is like a chocolate cake with a sugary icing", with an emoticon displaying a smiley face with tongue out.

"Gosh! It is not even safe to tweet something good, decent, and straight from the heart. Forget getting a reply or a retweet from some good folks. Instead, you get spam attacks with sexual undertones!" He was livid and was left so mystified with that uncomfortable post on his tweet that he failed to understand what on earth prompted such a reply to his harmless post.

"What the hell?" He screamed as he landed straight on his bed and buried his head into the pillow.

CHAPTER 6

With time, Rashv forgot his rejection as he involved himself in several activities. Soon, there was so much to do that his heart found breathing space to repair itself out and life started getting normal again. After several days of non-stop activity, he found a moment of solitude in his room and suddenly he realised how careless he had been and that there was so much to sort out in his room.

Rashv shut the door and stood there looking all over his room. For the first time in several days, he had a close look at his room and it seemed like a place which had suffered a nasty cyclone with everything strewn everywhere. Usually, Rashv's mom didn't come to his room during his vacations as per his pact with her.

"Thank God mom doesn't come here. Else she would have probably just choked to the putrid smell inside this room!" Rashv nodded his head sideways looking at the empty boxes of junk food strewn over the floor, his sweaty clothes lying randomly on the bed and dusty copies of old magazines lying carelessly stacked on the shelves. With such a setting, Rashv half-anticipated some weird things to happen during the night like the windows banging, his bedroom door creaking and eerie voices emanating from the ceiling as he stood there at the entrance, a silent and largely inactive witness of the entire mess. "Hello, Ramsay Brothers! My room beckons your attention as well!", he said as he decided to first clean his cupboard full of previous year's college books, files, a few souvenirs which he had received since his school days, fashion magazines and some other irrelevant stuff.

There was a huge stash of books to be lined up properly, old and used to be kept aside for the Raddiwala along with the old fashion magazines. He also wanted to make space for some more new books and magazines, all the important papers, souvenirs and newspaper cuttings of his favourite actresses and arrange them systematically rather than squishing them clumsily together in some corner and eventually making a complete mess out of it all.

Rashv meticulously picked up each piece of paper, folder, notes, old gifts and souvenirs. He stopped to look at them while recalling about where each of them was from. Some stuff was from long forgotten times and some memories felt like old friends, just as warm and comfortable. As he held his stuff in his hands and pressed down on the corners of the dog-eared books, certificates and cards, he smiled from the rush of old memories.

As he was rearranging his stuff, he came across mark sheets from his school days that were punched and stored into a file. As he flipped through them, memories of his school life flooded back and he recollected the excitement on his face at the time when he was being awarded the 'Consistent Performer' trophy on the last day of school as his rank was either 2nd or 3rd throughout his school life. Much to his dismay, he recalled that however much he tried, his rank neither improved nor deteriorated. He would never top, however hard he worked. Rather his rank would always be a rigid number of either 2nd or 3rd.

"Such is life. Here I have an entire shelf of trophies highlighted by this 'Consistent Performer' trophy and not even a single 'best performer' one even though I was one of the most studious pupils ever!", he sighed as he continued arranging things into his cupboard.

Rashv shook his head as if to shrug off the past and his gaze fell on something interesting. While putting aside his school file full of mark sheets, he noticed a few numbers placed at the top right corner of each mark sheet. "It must be the serial number", he thought. Rashv had a strange penchant for numbers. He would play with them, arrange them in as many permutations and combinations as he could and solve arithmetic puzzles for the sheer pleasure of logical analysis. And so, just for fun, Rashv added all the numbers placed at the top of every mark sheet and noted down the total. He did the same for each and every mark sheet that had been filed and the result left him astounded.

The numbers, when added yielded the same result on every mark sheet. 23!

Rashv blinked his eyes and even pinched himself just to make sure that he was not daydreaming. And he was not. He thought of doing the same for all of his college mark sheets and his excitement levels kept on increasing as he worked on the mark sheets like a mad scientist just on the verge of a path-breaking discovery. The modulation of his voice matched that of Arnab Goswami's in a debate on national television as he kept totaling the numbers and jotting the results serially and exclaiming a loud "Yes! Yes! Yes!" with every result. His empty mind was a playful devil's workshop and he chortled at each discovery. He didn't let his concentration wear off even though he heard his mom asking him to come downstairs.

"23 again! Oh Freak! This has to be directly from "Ripley's Believe It or Not!' Rashv exclaimed. "So will my mark sheets of the final year also total up to 23?" he chuckled in amusement.

Rashv pondered over it for a while with his heart jumping up and down like a kid's would at receiving his favourite toy. He inhaled and exhaled a few times so as to control his racing heart and decided to instead continue arranging things into his cupboard. Finally, the cupboard was taken care of in what was a never ending exercise with bitter-sweet memories of the past, taking Rashv down several memory lanes.

After spending his entire evening just cleaning and mopping

his room, he finally called it a day in the wonderful company of his mom and 'slouched into his bean bag with the latest issue of Vogue for his daily dose of gossip from the entertainment world. He hoped that it would keep him sane after all the astonishment he had experienced in the past few hours.

Rashv plugged his earphones into his Blackberry ignoring the blinking light of low battery that asked for his attention. He selected Michael Jackson's songs from his playlist to play in a loop. The beats started to create a peaceful harmony in his mind as he slowly flipped through the pages of Vogue and simultaneously made meticulous note of the latest trends in global fashion. The issue had images of female models along with a description each showcasing the latest trend in the bridal couture and instinctively he started giving them marks out of 10. Just as he was giving out the marks, Rashv stopped when his gaze fell on the image of his favourite female superstar labeled as "The Showstopper" dressed in probably one of the most stylish bridal dresses ever designed.

"Wow!" Rashv ogled at the picture and all of a sudden broke into an impromptu jig clutching at the magazine, her picture close to his chest as he danced his heart out till his quickening breath signaled him to stop and take a breather.

"I wish I get to dance with you in reality someday", he moaned as he closed his eyes and imagined them together, dancing as freely as they could while still clutching the magazine close to his chest as if he was in love.

"Knock knock,

Mind calling Heart, Mind calling Heart"

"What is it now?" asked the Heart.

"If wishes were horses, beggars would ride", sang the Mind swaying to its tune.

"Touché! Whatever!" scoffed the Heart. The mind reminding

the heart about the reality troubled the heart and it clanked onto the floor going into pieces.

Rashv kept the magazine aside and picked up the transparent cover in which it was delivered. He picked it up and stood looking at the cover in which he had just inserted the magazine.

The first line read as: 23, Rock Avenue.

He narrowed his eyes with brows coming together and stood there in silence without moving an inch. Each and every alphabet of the first line of the address resurfaced in front of his eyes over and over again.

Rashv gulped as he felt a hint of nervousness gnaw on him. He thought that it was some kind of a coincidence going on with him throughout the day but then as he dwelt on it some more, he realised that the repetitive sequence had actually been appearing in various ways for over four months now. At first, he recalled that he had attached no meaning to it whatsoever, but then he began to see way too many coincidences with the number involved. Like wherever he went, he noticed vehicles with license plates bearing the number 23 repetitively or in a special sequence and it was kind of surprising. It was either 2323 or 2332 or 2223 or 2324. Whenever he picked up the cell phone to see the time, it was xx: 23, their apartment was on the second floor, Door no. 32, again it was 23 written backwards, his birthday fell on 04.06.94 the sum of whose digits was 23, his roll number throughout his academic life was either 23 or some close number, mostly while reading he would stop at page number 23 or 32 or Chapter 23, especially these days and his uncle had bought a new SUV for which he had requested for the registration number 2323.. At first, he did not notice that the number had begun to appear around him but now his mind was running. Gosh! He blinked his eyes, took a pause, ran his tongue over his parched lips and recollected.

"My ranks during school were either 2nd or 3rd...

My roll number since the very beginning in college has been 23...

My favourite jerseys bear the same number... 23 - the one belonging to Michael Jordan, my icon!

Both the mobile numbers that are in use and the current one also possess the same number as the last two digits."

Rashv swallowed hard. Where was this leading to? Did it mean anything or was it only his mind playing games?

"Hold your horses Rashv, hold it before coming to any conclusion. There seems to be a bit more which is relatively suggestive in nature."

He removed the magazine from the cover and quickly flipped the pages to the desired page.

"Aah... here it is."

The showstopper's picture with badge no 23 and the page number.

The publisher's address...

Also, the number of missed calls by mom!"

Rashv stood there for a minute or two in awe of all the findings with his brain cells buzzing with a hint of strange possibility. He took a deep breath, ran his fingers through his hair and exclaimed with an ascending pitch of his voice, "All these findings mean that I may have some weird connection with the number TWENTY-THREE!"

CHAPTER 7

Rashv wrestled with his duvet as sleep eluded him for the night. It was nothing short of a ritual for him. On days when sleep was hard to come by, life's mysteries and other pertinent issues kept him wide awake. Today it was a number and he did not even know whether it was worth his worries or just a mere coincidence. TWENTY-THREE kept him occupied as he kept on looking out for various ways which could link him to the number. Failing to find any further explanations for the weird occurrence, Rashv concluded that maybe it would be good for him to just be on the right side of the number.

The next morning as the alarm clock buzzed off signaling a new day, Rashv laid flat on his back, pulled the blanket closer to him, and rested his left arm on his head. The raised arm gave a warning to his nostrils that 'a minute more in the position would most likely nauseate you and poison the air in the room.' He smiled at the odd realization, got up carelessly from the bed, and sprayed deodorant all over himself. The room smelled doubly mantastic with several sprays of his favourite deodorant and the lifeless jersey which Rashv had been wearing for over two days suddenly sprang back to life.

"Happy?" Rashv asked his flaring nostrils, twitching his nose to one side as he looked at himself in the mirror. The number twenty-three could be seen placed in a small size on the top left corner of his jersey. He beamed at the thought that something good with respect to friends or maybe even girlfriends would expectedly happen very soon in his mundane life. He smiled at the mirror and went back to bed again with the hope of getting a good sound sleep.

The next two days went on laboriously slow for Rashv as he took extra care to ensure that he included the number in all his activities. Quite funnily, he took to his new-found superstition by starting the day with drinking a glass of water in 23 sips, then switching the TV channel to 23 and viewing it the entire day to emphasize the good omen it represented. If that wasn't enough he even made Rahul spell out his name twenty-three times during a phone call. Also, he went to sleep sharp at 23:00 hours and woke up the next morning without even blinking an eyelid during his sleep. In short, he did all kinds of weird things, even things he had never done before; only to be on the right side of the number and all in strange hope for some angel to drop from the sky and make his living world happening and full of life. And in the meantime, days flew by swiftly with now only two days left for his classes to commence.

For the most part of the final day too, the number was on his mind. It filled him with a new-found exhilaration. Somehow, it felt like he had found the key to success in Life. But at the same time, his grey cells were buzzing with curious thoughts. There had to be more facets to this rare occurrence.

It somehow feels more than a superstition. Like more than just an oddity. As time went on, the initial excitement of spotting a pattern in his life wore off and he became more and more curious to know as to why the number 23 was repeatedly occurring in his life and if it meant anything. Why 23? Did it hold a message? Could life really be predicted to run around a number?

Finally, he took to the internet for answers. He tried random search phrases on Google and the direct query of "What does the number 23 mean?" returned several funny answers by the mighty search engine. He clicked open the first link.

"The number 23 in itself does not mean anything other than denoting the mathematical connotation that it is greater than the number 22 and less than 24", he chuckled. "Clever! But too objective for my purpose." As he clicked on the other search results thrown by Google, he came across several interesting references indicating the different ways the number was integrated into the fabric of human life. Excitingly, it seemed to be everywhere!

He continued reading...

"The average lifespan of a human being is 63 years or roughly 23,000 days."

"The average Human physical biorhythm lasts for 23 days."

"Each parent contributes 23 chromosomes to the start of a human life. The nuclei of cells in humans have 46 chromosomes occurring in 23 pairs."

"In humans, the 23rd chromosomal pair determines the gender of the foetus."

"It takes an average of 23 seconds for human blood to complete a single circulation in adults."

"The Earth's angle of rotation is off by 23.5 degrees."

"The Tropic of Cancer is at 23.5 degrees N latitude."

"The Tropic of Capricorn is at 23.5 degrees S latitude."

"The Mayans believed that the world would end on December 23rd, 2012. (20+1+2 = 23)"

"There are more UFO sightings on July 23rd than on any other day of the year."

"Darwin's Origin of Species was published in 1859 (1+8+5+9=23)"

"The 23rd number of the English alphabet is W, which has 2 ends down and 3 ends up."

"The letter W is located between the numerals 2 and 3 on your keyboard."

"The number of times Caesar was stabbed to death."

"The numbers 4, 8, 15, 16, 23 and 42 are explained as human factors of the Valencetti Equation which is believed to predict the date of extinction of the human race."

"Rotation period of asteroids is at least 2.3 hours. A rotation period less than this would cause them to be torn apart."

"The number is one of the 'Lost' cursed numbers from the hit TV Show 'Lost'."

The theme of the number 23 was also seen to have been predominantly featured in his favourite movies too: Serendipity, Futurama, Star Wars: A New hope, Life of Brain, Seinfeld, The Matrix Reloaded, Die Hard III, The Big Lebowski and many other movies.

"A good number of great athletes who have seen immense success have worn the number 23. Michael Jordan, David Beckham, Steve Waugh, LeBron James, Ryne Sandberg, Don Mattingly..."

"The Atomic Bomb (U-235 – the Uranium isotope used in bombs consists of the number 23 and 5 which is a combination of digits in the number 23) was dropped on Hiroshima, Japan at 8:15 (8+15 = 23) on 06.08.1945."

"The Birthday Paradox states that a group of any randomly selected 23 people is the lowest number of people where the probability is more than 50% that they would share the same birthday."

"Numerous people have claimed to see the number 23 everywhere prior to enormous successes or failures."

"23 enigmas, an esoteric belief that all incidents and events are directly connected to the number 23, some permutation of the number 23 or a number related to 23", "Wow! That's exactly what's happening with me!" his interest shot up and he kept looking on for more facts.

A link from a popular esoteric site returned the following message, which had him literally jumping up and down... "Angel Number 23: Message from the angels – 'This is a message from your spiritual guides, who can see that the answer to your prayers is now within reach. They encourage you to stay positive to ensure that you attract the best possible outcome."

He surfed the web and was also led to several further references to concepts in Numerology, Symbolism and Astrology. Even though he did understand too much from it at all, from one page to another he got the singular message that the number is considered to be as one of the most significant numbers in the number system. Everywhere he read, he found connotations and references to success, fame and Divine help related to the number. It filled him with the positive expectation that everything was finally going to work out for the best in his life very soon as the number was appearing in his own life everywhere he looked.

Apparently, this was to be one of the most significant discoveries of his life thus far, and as we would soon see, a sagacious accident of things that he was not in the quest of.

"Life is due for some changes" He smiled and turned off the system. That night he had the most peaceful sleep he had had in ages.

CHAPTER 8

Rashv sprang up from his daily slumber of 5 hours (because you know it! The sum of digits in 23 was 5), spanked the alarm clock, stretched his arms, flexed his nonexistent muscles and yawned twice before abandoning the duvet and rushed towards his mom's room.

She was calm and lay cuddled to the blanket when Rashv banged open the door, gave the alarm clock a peculiar 'meh' look as there was still some time before mom would get up, shrugged his shoulders and tried to shake her up from her slumber.

"Two minutes, Rashv!" she pleaded and turned and adjusted her blanket.

He let out a long trailing 'Hmmm' and left for his daily regime. After almost an hour Rashv emerged from his room wearing a grey jersey, of course bearing the number 23 and black jeans, his dark curly hair neatly done with a spray of serum, his black oval shaped metal frame fashionably rested on the rim of his nose and a generous spray of cologne that he sprayed all over himself, probably emptying half of the can.

"Good Morning!" Rashv's mom was seated on one of the chairs across the small dining table. "So, all set for the first day, the first time in coaching classes, young guy?"

Rashv beamed at his mom with his rotund cheeks stretching as far as the size of a six-door limousine and took the chair opposite his mom's. could see the rising formations of vapors from the piping hot plate of samosas taking various shapes in the air as he pounced on them. "If there's Heaven, it's here, mmmm..." he dramatized as he took the first bite of the hot samosa. Sensing it too hot to eat, he quite predictably now, carefully cut the samosas into 23 pieces, waited for a few minutes for them to cool down, and then gorged upon them with some tomato sauce and garlic chutney that further enhanced the taste. All this while his mom looked at him with her 'look-at-him-he's-the-apple-of-my-eyes' look, with her eyes showering all the motherly love that she could upon him as if Rashv was still a baby getting ready to attend pre-school for the first time. Within minutes Rashv was ready to leave with his backpack full of books when his mom sprang to life from her trance of sending off Rashv to pre school when he was all tears, sad and had managed a typical melodrama just like his peers.

"Wait! Just have this spoonful of curd. It acts as Shagun and it is always better to have it before starting anything as auspicious as your studies for the first year." She announced and dashed a spoonful into his mouth.

"Mom, can I take some for my friends too?" Rashv almost pleaded for it.

And almost immediately his mom emptied the entire bowl of curd into an air-tight Tupperware container and shoved it safely into one of the corners of his huge backpack.

"There you go!" exclaimed his mom before bidding him goodbye.

"Bye, Mom!", Rashv reciprocated with a quick wave of his hand and stepped out of the house. He looked at his wrist watch and the display brought a big smile on his face. It read as 5:23 am. "Good time to start off!", he smiled affirmatively. It strengthened his hope that everything was going to be fine.

Seeing Rashv all smiles and in a raring-to-go mood, his mom felt relieved that she did not have to resort to her customary motivational 'Life, Setbacks and Winnings' session again.

Rashv reached the institute almost 30 minutes prior to the commencement of the lectures. "Damn! There's no one around. Not even the support staff, the professors, or the students. Even the doors are locked. What am I supposed to do in the meanwhile?" He stood there in dark for a while probably amused by the idea of having to resort to coaching institutes for the first time in life, BBM-ed Rahul about having reached and finally having nothing to do, he started crushing candies on his Blackberry Z10 smartphone with the phone volume set to full.

Within no time, hordes of people started coming in with the peon opening the doors, followed by two professors and then students of varying intellects which was as varying as the fragrance that they each wore. Sliding his smartphone into his front pocket trouser, he stood beside the peon holding the Tupperware container in his hands. The peon who was standing in front of the classroom gate with a paper in his hand gave him a look of despise but Rashv smiled and offered him a spoonful of curd. He ignored him initially but eventually agreed. He took the spoonful into his palm first and then into his mouth. He licked the remaining curd left on his palm, gave a satisfactory smile to Rashv, looked into the paper, and started calling out the names of the students.

Everyone took a spoonful and entered the classroom with the sweet shagun in their mouths. While a majority of them took it sportingly without creating much fuss about it, although reluctantly, some took it with a sneer on their faces. Even the two professors took a spoonful from Rashv and thanked him for his gesture.

Just then, the peon announced the name of a girl called Beenal. But no one turned up. The peon called out for Beenal again. In a short while, a young bewitching girl with a charming face, long straightened hair left open, neatly dressed in a cool blue tee and a matching pair of denim appeared in front of them while uttering some last goodbye words over a phone call.

Rashv was left open mouthed when he saw Beenal. He was

left mesmerized by her sheer presence and immediately his heart prodded his brain to wake up, break the ice and make friends with her. Err... No. He would try for 'Good friends'. But just as Rashv was about to speak and introduce himself, Beenal took the opportunity to speak out first.

"What?" She hissed in an angry tone which was on a rather high pitch thus attracting the attention of the fellow students while looking directly into Rashv's eyes. The peon and the two professors stood their respective grounds acting indifferent to what was happening.

He was dejected and his heart felt like it had been mercilessly crushed under the burden of her piercing heels and buried deep under the ground.

"I'd like to offer you a spoonful of curd as shagun before starting our studies" Rashv replied, coming out of the spell that she had cast upon him.

She scanned him. Up and down from head to toe; not once but twice.

"It seems you have left your occasionally functional brain at home. Kindly carry it henceforth so that you realise that this is not your momma's kindergarten school where you are trying to please everybody by behaving like a stupid teenager looking for attention. Grow up!" She protested and stormed off, refusing to take any of the curd.

His heart was left devastated as he had not expected such a hostile reaction from her. He was stupefied momentarily as the remaining students simply walked into the classroom giving him a sideways glance, some pitying him, some laughing their hearts out at the situation.

"What gets sold first? The look, the presentation, the way you talk and carry yourself or the good and noble intentions that you have?" Rashv thought standing there in silence as he took in what had just happened with him.

THE 23RD GIRL

Amidst all the disorder with almost everyone mocking Rashv with sarcastic jokes and loud cheer, Rashv took the vacant first-row bench. His movements seemed mechanical. He was yet to recover from the storm that had inadvertently hit his feelings. Soon the professor walked in and silence resumed.

The lecture began on a fun note with the students introducing themselves with a line or a quote at the end. The activity started with lots of excitement as each and everyone started introducing themselves one after another starting from the last row. And all of a sudden, the professor called out for Beenal to introduce herself. She stood up with a tinge of a wicked smile forming on her face.

"Everyone knows me here. What's there to introduce?" Beenal argued with the professor who seemed to be adamant, nodding his head from left to right. "There is someone present in this class who still doesn't know you. So kindly go ahead and introduce yourself to the class.", asserted the professor with his eyes on Rashv.

Left with no choice, Beenal rose to her feet and reluctantly introduced herself.

"I am a bee that stings rarely but very harshly", she began with her eyes fixated at Rashv. This was met with lots of fake coughing from her classmates along with a long trailing sound of 'Hmm...'. Beenal let out a smile and continued.

"Hello everyone, I am Beenal. My surname is not as important as my name and who I am. I aspire to be a Teacher and perhaps the first thing I would teach my students would be to not come off as goody-two-shoes especially in their very first encounter with me if nothing else", she bragged with a smile that seemed to be mocking Rashv comprehensively.

Everyone's eyes widened as she kept on taking pot shots on Rashv. Someone from the far end even whistled which led to a huge roar of claps from her classmates.

"Okay. That was wonderful", interjected the professor on top of his voice in a bid to end the brouhaha and signaled Beenal to take her seat.

Seated on the first bench, Rashv was taking in all that Beenal had to say with a straight face as he sat through it all immobile, giving an impression that he was least interested in what she had to say or rather towards her mean introduction.

"And now", continued the professor looking at Rashv. "It is your turn, young man, to introduce yourself to the others present in the class." Even though Rashv wasn't looking directly towards the professor, he clearly understood to whom the professor was referring.

Rashv rose from his perch and turned around to face the class. His eyes kept looking for Beenal and there he noticed her, seated next to the wall, resting her back, with her head held high and wearing her trademark 'I-am-the-queen' expression on her face.

Upon seeing her, Rashv's lips automatically widened into the sweetest smile which could have stirred up even the most passive person. Instead, Beenal turned her gaze away from him.

Rashv cleared his throat and started.

"Hello friends! I am Rashv, meaning a Symbol of Love." He continued further, "I possess the capability to turn a cynical person into a believer of Love", he stated with a raised right brow and a glee on his face. The class along with the professor were left stunned with the way in which he explained his name. Their dazed faces showed the ambiguity their mind was in. They were unable to conclude from his explanation whether he was a born genius or simply an idiot.

"That was profound!" exclaimed the professor breaking the silence.

Unwilling to stop at that, Rashv continued with his so called awesomeness that was oozing out of him with his cheeks all flushed. "Also, I am a practitioner of the thought process that, 'The happiness of your life depends on the quality of your thoughts and I have been practicing it for years'', he quipped with a grin on his face, looked towards Beenal for once and took his seat.

The class erupted with a simultaneous 'Ohhs' with everyone looking towards Beenal for a probable reaction to what Rashv just said in the end.

"Will you all be kind enough to listen to this qualified teacher for once and not to the ones who are building castles in the air?" the professor broke in signaling an end to the fun banter and entertainment and the commencement of some serious studies.

Beenal was seething with anger. She swore to God that she would give Rashv a befitting reply and was desperately waiting for the lecture to get over to be able to finally confront him. Whereas, on the other hand, Rashv sat amicably with his eyes and ears glued to what the professor was explaining while his heart thanked the professor for giving him a small opportunity to settle scores. And amidst all this, his heart managed to do a small victory lap before focusing back on the white board.

The lecture got over way early than the scheduled time of three hours. As soon as he sensed that the professor was going to end the lecture and call it a day, Rashv packed his bag and took the very first opportunity to sprint out of the classroom before Beenal could. He took two steps at a time while going down the staircase so that he could be quickly out of her sight and thus avoid any further verbal confrontations with her. She was capable of 'stinging hard'. He was sure of atleast this much about her.

That afternoon as Rashv took to brushing up the day's lessons, he sat with a goal and a target on his mind. But little did he know that his goals would be too difficult to achieve. Flashes of Beenal's attractive face and her thick bangs caressing her face kept his heart occupied while his brain continuously kept requesting him to concentrate on his books instead.

CHAPTER 9

"Knock Knock, Mind calling Heart, Mind calling Heart."

The Mind prodded the Heart once more. And yet again it met with the same result.

"Fine, keep making up various scenarios in your head with that girl who doesn't even want to be friends with you. And let me also warn you that this is one sided love. if at all it can be called love!" his brain hissed.

La la la la la ... his heart swirled in a dance, completely ignoring the brain's advice as Rashv kept on staring at the outside world through the window and imagining himself with Beenal. The way her mysterious eyes looked at him, her vibrant voice and the way she flicked her hair with a slight jerk to her head was enough for Rashv to fall head over heels in love with her.

His condition was no different during the night. Sleep eluded him again for the better part of the night. For the n-th time, he wrestled with the duvet, tossing and turning from left to right. Beenal had completely taken over his mind and the much-needed sleep that he required kept eluding him as he stared, sometimes at the rotating fan, sometimes at the flapping curtains and sometimes at the Deepika Padukone poster that he had pasted on one of the walls of his room. "Naah... she looks prettier than you!", He closed his eyes and clutching the duvet closer to his chest, sang "I am in Love, I am in Love...", with a shy smile crossing his lips.

Although he hit the bed sharp at 23:00 hours, sleep beckoned him way after the midnight. He was burning a different kind of midnight oil that only lovers burn. His blooming one-sided love for Beenal kept him awake just as the case was with all his previous encounters and interactions with his one-sided love interests. But there was one difference that separated this experience from his past encounters. It was his new-found fascination with the number 23. And more importantly the fact that the number was working in his favor these days gave a much-needed boost to his ever-dwindling confidence and brought a kind of spark, a zest in his life that was missing until this realization.

The next morning began on a pretty awful note for him. He woke up later than his scheduled span of five hours with his head spinning like a rotating top that the Generation X played with during their childhood.

"Did the earth just wobble?"

"No, you idiot. It is you who is wobbling from a lack of sleep", replied the brain to the heart.

Somehow, he managed to finish his daily routine, freshen up, and got ready wearing another jersey, washed and ironed, bearing the magic number 23.

"Good Morning, Mom!" Rashv wished her mom back as he wiped off the last traces of sleep in his tired eyes and sat across the table for his breakfast.

A few minutes later his Z10 beeped with a series of messages from Rahul.

"I am stuck in the loo, terrible pain. The Passage seems to be blocked. Won't be able to come today."

Rashv laughed his heart out as he visualized Rahul sitting on the commode with various types of sounds - sometimes in desperation and sometimes a feel good one emanating from his vocal chords.

"Haha... May Lord give you the strength of The Himalayas in such testing times", he promptly replied him, even placing a couple of winking eye emoticons before sending it across to Rahul.

Rashv reached the coaching institute with love songs tickling his imagination. Seated on one of the steps of the first-floor classroom, he waited anxiously for everyone to bring in their groggy, early morning faces and to give his imagination the loveliest company, Beenal was there with him in his shy thoughts with the two of them dancing to some of the most romantic numbers either on a sun-kissed hilltop or in a desert or under the moonlight, Bollywood style.

The peon was the first to arrive. For a second he seemed a bit scared to see someone wildly swaying their head from side to side. Probably it was the hood of Rashv's jacket that covered his face completely which got him scared for a moment. Rashv was so lost that he didn't even realise that the peon was bending himself down to look at his face.

"Ah! The curd is here", the Peon sighed fearing another one of those frightening experiences. "Just as I thought, he's a lunatic", he muttered under his breath. "You come too early for the classes", he declared as he went about performing his daily routine of preparing the room for the classes. As he opened the doors of the classroom, the loud squeaky sound made by opening the doors broke Rashv's reverie all of a sudden and he came to know of the peon's presence. They eyed each other. Rashv acknowledged him with a small smile while entering the classroom.

He took the first-row bench, put his mobile on silent mode, unplugged the earphones from his ears and began to revise the previous day's lessons. Soon, his fellow classmates started coming in and occupying the vacant benches. All through the while, he looked at everyone walking in with a cross eye, in anticipation of seeing Beenal walk through and grace his sight with her lovely face. He sat all edgy with his eyes yearning for her. But alas, he had to settle without one as it looked like there were no signs of her coming for the lecture.

Days passed by with Rashv enjoying the company of his new friends on one hand and aching for Beenal's attention on the other. Meanwhile, Beenal was still keeping a distance from Rashv. Rashv simply could not understand the reason behind this royal ignore as it continued for several days. He would daydream about her throughout the day and weave beautiful dreams of them together in the night, only to find them strewn over hopelessly the next morning with her "I-don't-give-a-damn-to-you" attitude.

He persisted to believe in his theory of number 23 for days but somewhere he felt that somehow it was not working in her case. His hopes of striking a meaningful conversation with Beenal had now started to fade; forget even expecting a friendship with her. Rashv started focussing on his studies as much as he could to divert his attention from her thoughts. He also had to go through another of his mom's monotonous 'Life, Setbacks and Winning' sessions as his semester tests were barely a week away.

But little did he know what was going to happen... very soon.

CHAPTER 10

The sun blared through the crystal clear sky at the world down below. The trees looked exhausted and parched from the beaming sun rays. The radiating heat had almost created an atmosphere of a hot oven. It was one of the most horrible summer days one had witnessed in recent years. Rashv took a step out of his home and made way towards the institute for his class test.

Even in such an awful weather the street was bustling with hordes of people who had to stay out to earn their living. Vegetable vendors were sweating it out in order to earn the day's bread, young professionals hopped in and popped out of buses, taxis and autos, probably rushing for client meetings and delivery boys rode hurriedly to their destinations. Rashv was amused to see lots of people on the street take the 'Bake Me' challenge in the sweltering summer heat.

Just then a rush of air followed a passing bus. Rashv felt like he had suddenly taken a plunge into a cool lake to beat the summer heat. He had been trying to hail an auto but not even a single one was stopping by. He looked here and there in desperation for any signs of a vacant auto and luckily one of them finally stopped right in front of him. Just as he was about to lift his leg and settle inside, a sharp pullback by the top handle of his bag took him aback. The effect of this sudden pull was such that his right leg got stuck and trapped inside the autorickshaw while the rest of his body was pulled outside the auto. In a way, he was left to balance on his left foot.

"What the..."

"I had hailed it first!", snapped a brusque voice before Rashv could complete his sentence.

With contempt in his eyes, he turned his face to his left to find none other than Beenal, one hand holding a couple of books close to her chest and a long tote bag hanging from the same shoulder. The contempt in his eyes immediately vanished in the air upon seeing her angry, red face and instead a tinge of smile appeared on his face. She carried a somewhat drained look. Either she was exhausted due to the heat or was plainly irritated due to the stress related to the test, Rashv tried to reason.

"Rashv? You?" squeaked a stupefied Beenal. Her decibel levels got raised by a notch as even in the wildest of her dreams she had not expected to meet Rashv like this. Meanwhile, he somehow managed to bring both his legs back to the common ground.

"Hey Beenal!" he beamed.

Beenal responded with a not-so-happy-to-see-you 'Hello' and jumped into the auto without caring to have a second glance at him.

Rashv stood there, his feet rooted to the ground as his heart took its own sweet little time to adjust to her unexpected presence.

"Rashv!" Beenal snorted not once but twice but he chose to continue with his daydreaming. "Do you want to get in the auto or should I leave?" Beenal gritted in a slow intimidating voice.

Rashv could simply nod his head and got into the auto obeying her like a child. He still couldn't believe his luck. Beenal was actually asking him to sit in the auto with him. He turned around his cap bearing the number 23 so as to acknowledge the positive role the number was probably again playing in his life. He took a large sip of water and offered it to Beenal who replied with a stark no.

"What's with so much of arrogance? Why is she always so rude?" Rashv thought as both of them looked in the opposite direction without caring to utter a single word.

Upon reaching the center, Rashv being the thorough gentleman he was, paid the bill and both of them got off from the auto. Barely fifteen minutes were left for the test to commence and a majority of the students had arrived. Heads turned upon seeing both of them arrive together.

"Just how?" one of his friends pulled him to his side and whispered.

"Don't read anything much into it. It means nothing at all!" Rashv replied with a slight awkwardness which quickly turned into bitterness as he looked at Beenal who just walked past him and took a separate seat. He took his cap off and put it in his backpack.

The students were divided into two classrooms with only three students on every bench. Rashv walked in calm and composed, ignoring the heart and listening to his brain. As he walked in, he witnessed complete chaos with someone shouting and a majority of students scurrying through some last minute revision of formulae and notes. Rashv stood there in amusement for he didn't understand this last minute studying just before an exam or for that matter even a test. For him, exams and tests were just other days in his life as he was always well prepared in advance for any such tests.

And at that juncture, the invigilator walked in asking the students to settle down. Rashv waited for them to settle so as to take a vacant seat but not a single seat was available. As a result, he checked another classroom and took the vacant corner seat of the first bench. He prepared his desk armed with a pen, pencil, ruler, and calculator for the accounting test. Just then another invigilator dropped in and signaled the class to take their respective seats and keep the books and bags in front of the whiteboard.

Rashv closed his eyes, took a deep breath, and got ready to nail the questions that were to be presented in a few minutes from now. But something strange happened. Unsure, he blinked his eyes, once more and again. It was Beenal. Beenal had taken a seat next to him on the first-row bench!

He couldn't believe his luck for the second time in the day.

Beenal gave him a slight smile while still continuing to avoid any interactions with him. It was a mixed signal which Rashv carefully ignored and chose to focus on the test itself. Meanwhile, the invigilator started distributing the answer sheets amidst pin-drop silence. But Rashv was damn sure that if his heart beat any harder everyone else would come to know about it. The ringing of the bell, loud and sharp broke his tension as the three-hour sprint began. The long test paper drained the energy of the students. Rashv attempted the entire set of questions with ease although with a slight amount of distraction coming in from the presence of Beenal next to him.

Rashv was all pumped up with an adrenaline rush seeping through him as the students started discussing the question paper. "No, no. This is the correct answer. My balance sheet got tallied", he was excitedly discussing the test paper with one of his friends as they started to make a move from the classroom. Rashv was all gaga and from what he had heard from others, the paper seemed to be just fine and nothing extraordinary and it seemed like there was a good chance for him to ace the test. And in all this excessive enthusiasm came a sudden sound that startled them all.

Rashv had been standing at the edge of the staircase and in his enthusiasm of discussing the answers; he missed the first step of the staircase thereby landing on his bottom crossing a series of almost ten stairs in one go. Beenal was standing at the end of the staircase with one of her friends. She could not control her laughter and soon many others joined her in a cacophonous laughter. Rashv sat there rubbing his lower back for a moment. He went numb for a minute or so as his heart started pounding, probably yet to take in what had just happened, with a bit of difficulty in breathing causing a slight stomach distress.

He somehow managed to get up with a helpful hand from Rahul and quickly vacated the premises ignoring the pain that was straining his movement.

"Why are you in such a hurry?" Rahul questioned.

"Where the hell were you? You were supposed to meet me here before the start of the test, weren't you?" Rashv asked him instead of answering Rahul.

"I called you man. Your phone was constantly unavailable!", Rahul replied in a slightly irritated tone.

"What?" he panicked and started searching his trouser pockets for his smartphone and they turned out empty apart from his handkerchief. He also looked for it in his bag but to no avail. "Damn! I have lost my phone." he squealed with disappointment written all over his face.

"In the Auto! I must have lost it in the Autorickshaw!" Rashv added as an afterthought. "Aaargghhh!" he screamed. "Mom is going to kill me!s", he gulped as they waited for an auto to take them home safely, Rashv in particular.

At home, as Rashv massaged his lower back with a bag of hot water, the sounds of contemptuous laughter ricocheted in his ears. He was hurt with the way everyone had laughed at him and more so Beenal. He had not expected Beenal to laugh the most at his fall. She came across as being totally insensitive towards his agony. Thankfully, he had some respite as he was saved from his mom's anger over losing his smartphone, mainly because of the injuries he had sustained.

At night he found it difficult to sleep as his sore muscles kept him awake. Eventually, he took to the window, laid himself in an armchair and looked outside at the world down below. The street was bustling with traffic and youngsters could be seen laughing around with their friends and there were lovers enjoying the cool breeze either gazing at the stars in the moonlit sky or walking with their hands entwined.

"Lovers!" he sighed as his thoughts drifted towards Beenal, once again. He thought about the past few months when he had first met Beenal and how his relationship had evolved with her ever since. It was an acrimonious relationship from day one and the bitterness between them had gradually grown over petty quarrels. It had overall been pretty one-sided for Rashv and the faint glimmer of hope kindled by her interactions during the day was eventually put out by the way she had mocked at him when he had fallen from the stairs.

"Girls are so difficult to understand. You never know what's cooking in their minds!" Rashv mused shaking his head. He realised that understanding her mind probably wasn't as easy as solving accounting problems. Leaving it at there, he got up from the armchair. His sprained muscles could not bear any more strain from sitting in it for too long. He walked up to the refrigerator to feed his low-spirited, famished self some well-deserved sundae. Ice cream tubs are always good company to a punctured self-esteem.

The next morning Rashv was surprisingly in pretty high spirits, oozing with confidence. The pain from the fall had reduced to a fair extent. The results of the accounting test were also expected that day and he was pretty sure that he would have aced it. Rahul met him midway and both of them left together for the coaching institute.

The students started pouring in as both of them sat beside each other and chatted animatedly. It was like a complete fish market with almost everyone greeting each other as if they were meeting after a long time. Such is the exuberance of youth, full of madness.

Just then the professor walked in with bundles of answer sheets in his hands and started distributing them randomly among the students. "The answer sheets are being distributed randomly. Each student will read the name on the sheet, the marks, and the remark on the answer sheet before passing on the answer sheet to the concerned student. This will be done until everyone gets their answer sheet. And we will start from the one seating on the last bench to the right."

There was a lot of nervousness on everyone's faces. Some were happy. Some were dejected with the marks and the remarks awarded to them. And after waiting for almost 30 minutes it was Rashv's turn. He stood up, turned around the answer sheet and gasped seeing the name. Not knowing how to react to it, he straightforwardly announced the name and marks of the student without letting his expressions change even a bit. "Beenal, 96/100, keep it up!" After all, he wasn't able to forget how she mocked at him when he fell down the stairs yesterday. The entire class gave out a series of claps before Rashv could even pass the sheet towards her. He looked around in search of Beenal and there she was, seated on the front seat of the middle row. She seemed to be very happy. After what seemed like ages the resounding claps died out. It was Beenal's turn now and she observed the name and the marks and bursted out laughing leaving the entire class bemused. She stopped immediately, cleared her throat, and read the markings from the answer sheet that she had in her hands.

"Rashv, 69/100, lack of concentration and silly mistakes."

The class was left dumbstruck and so was Rashv. Neither he nor the class including the professor could believe his low score.

The activity concluded soon and a dejected Rashv took the very first opportunity to rush back home and analyze his mistakes. As he was rushing out, he was stopped midway by Beenal.

"Hey! Rashv! Look I'm very sorry for my behaviour

yesterday. I shouldn't have laughed the way I did and should have been a bit more sensitive. But nevertheless, please accept my apologies and forgive me!", she pleaded with puppy eyes. "Here, this is for you", she insisted putting out her right hand in front of him. "Consider this as a gift from my end to put an end to our acrimonious relationship."

Still in deep shock over the result and with his mind unable to comprehend what was going on, Rashv took the box wrapped in shining silver paper into his hands.

"Open the gift please", she teased him and came a bit closer towards him.

Boom!!!

A spring boxing glove sprang out of the box which shook the broad daylights out of Rashv, pushing him two steps backward, reeling in pain, his head spinning like a top and the sudden impact leaving him with a swollen nose.

"Ahh... Carefully! Anyway, don't miss the curd around the box, sweetie!" she blurted and gave her up-to-no-good smile and left, leaving Rashv all to himself, stupefied, livid, agitated, as well as humiliated - all at the same time.

CHAPTER 11

"The only thing worse than a recipient of a royal ignore is the recipient of an agonizingly given royal ignore." Rashv mused nursing his nose with an ice pack as he locked himself in his room. Just yesterday he was soothing his stiff muscles with a hot water bag and today he was putting ice packs on his brand new injury. He convulsed at the thought of having been at the receiving end of so much insult in a matter of just two days.

Rashv took one large sip of fresh lime and spoke under his breath. "It was so cruel of you Beenal to have thoroughly enjoyed my suffering, especially the ones you have inflicted upon me for God knows what reason." He spoke in a soft and disheartened tone as he took a momentary look at the spring boxing glove placed on his study table.

"Brain, where are you?" asked the battered heart. "When I didn't want any of your advice you were always on the jump, peppering me with your sound and distinguished advice. Now when I need you the most, there is no response from you!" It snarled.

"I had warned you well in advance. But you didn't pay any heed to my advice", hissed the brain.

"So, what? That's not a good enough excuse for not helping me out when I am in my most dire state", wept the incorrigible heart. It had simply been a one-sided love affair or rather a half love and Rashv realized that he had been played along by her all this while. He felt embarrassed as he realised that over the past few days, he had been acting like a love struck puppy eyeing every opportunity to have her attention. Not knowing what to make out of the whole situation, he took out his answer sheet and carefully observed the mistakes that had been highlighted.

"Hmm... It's true I made some really silly mistakes in the paper. What had come over me!" he grimaced and recollected the vague memories of her expressions in his mind. Realizing that he had again begun to think of her, he snarled and tried to distract his mind from her thoughts. Just then his mom entered the room with a bowl of pasta. "Here, have some pasta with a cup of your favourite Latte", she insisted and pushed the mug and bowl in front of him.

"Thank you, Mom. This is exactly what I needed right now", Rashv replied without an iota of contentment on his face. His mom helped him divert his mind as she recounted gossips from the day. Her stories lasted for what seemed like dawn to dusk. The long chit-chat with his mom helped him to relax and gave him a much-needed breather and he forgot the heart sore that he felt from the happenings over the past few days. He flexed his nonexistent muscles and gave a signal to his mom that he needed to retire for the evening.

"Life... just when you manage to find a way to deal with it, it changes course suddenly, forcing you to mend your ways accordingly. But I guess it is now time to forge my own path and stop meandering along its continuously changing path", he mused ruefully. "When I was totally ignorant about the number 23 and the meaning it held in my life, the number seemed to be playing its part to perfection. But just when I realized its significance and started to meticulously plan my life around it, it stopped showing its magic. Somewhere it did ditch me. But now it's time to take things completely under my own control", he felt a surge of confidence as he decided to take his life in his own hands. Rashv sprang from his passive state. It was like as if something had struck him at the core. He felt as if a new wisdom had dawned upon him, enlightening him to move to a brand new reality and direction in life.

"It is time to take life head-on without allowing it to take me for a free ride all the time", he announced as he thanked

Beenal for the way she had treated him. He thanked her for
having inadvertently brought a new clarity in his life. Good
days follow hard times. He reminded himself. And this was
surely going to be the start of a good time in his life, he
decided as he descended the stairs towards his room, with a
new spring in his steps, as he hummed a perfect rendition of
Bon Jovi's 'It's My Life.'

The only thing that had been lacking in Rashv's life was body
confidence. Despite being at the top of the pile in academics,
he found himself amounting to lesser than what he would
have liked when it came to attention from the opposite sex.
All his academic excellence could not add up to a confident
personality. Having suffered the ignominy of endless
rejections and repeated jabs at his self-confidence and riding
on a new found wave of self-assurance, he decided to get
even with fate and play a strange game involving himself and
his obsession with the ruling number of his life - 23.

It would appear to be a bit unreasonable to the reader but
revenge does make it difficult to see or reason out clearly;
especially when one is young and inexperienced. It is indeed
the endless hope and invincibility of teenage that makes one
assume that all ideas and dreams, however unreasonable, are
within their reach. It was the same hopefulness that triggered
a knee-jerk reaction in him which made him decide that he
had now had enough rejections in his life and that now,
getting even with his hurt would mean that he would
befriend, date and ditch 22 girls in all and settle with the 23rd
girl who came into his life. In deciding to do so he thought
that he would have some semblance of control over his own
destiny. To keep a score of the number of girls he met as a
part of his strange plan, he thought that it would be proper
that he should receive a gift or some souvenir as a token of
affection and remembrance from each girl who would
amount to a significant place in his life including the ones he
would date and later ditch. A satisfied smile came across his

lips as he imagined himself as a heartbreaker and for once, as the guy who had some choice about how things turned out in his life.

Rashv picked up the glove box from his study table and smiled as he placed it on one of the empty shelves designated for the purpose. It would be the souvenir from Beenal, he decided. He dived into his memories and fished his personal stuff for souvenirs from other girls. As he walked down the dusty lanes of memory he found more such stuff to be placed on the shelf. He found cards from his childhood friend Priya who had moved to a different town when they were just 10 and he remembered how teary eyed they both were at the unavoidable parting; a small teddy bear keychain from that weird bespectacled friend in school who built a science project for him and submitted on his behalf when he got punished in class for having taking it all lightly... he always thought she had a crush on him but he could never reciprocate enough; a compilation of English pop music from his crush in mid-school from the days when he had not confessed his love to her, the small red plastic flower from Heta that she had given him on the Annual Traditional Day at college. Sigh! Artificial flowers don't change. They remain attractive forever but are of little value. Just like Heta had been for him. Beautiful and unavailable!

As he arranged the gifts and remembered the friendships and the hurt from the past, he let out a wicked smile out of an odd sense of satisfaction at having given a start to a frantic meet-date-breakup scenario. The other commitment he made to himself was that in doing all of this, his studies would not be compromised.

Indeed, sometimes in life, you find yourself in the middle of nowhere, and sometimes in the middle of that nowhere you find the answers to the questions that are troubling you.

CHAPTER 12

After what seemed like hours, Rashv emerged from his room and sank in favorite red bean bag in front of the idiot box.

"So you finally got time for me after so many days", fretted the bean bag as it gave away under Rashv's weight. Just a week remained for the college to commence the first class of the final year and Rashv was in no mood to take up books into his hands, just yet. Instead, he preferred to spend his time sleeping, eating, and playing counter strike on his PC.

"Mom?"

"I think you should begin taking your own resolutions seriously, Son", quipped his mom before Rashv could say anything further. "There is always a first time for everything and I think it's time you should think about your health too and hit the gym. And anyways before you flare up again let me tell you that I am only asking you to do this for your own benefit as I have got nothing to gain from it." His mom had the look of a slight dejection on her face.

"Ok. Ok! Don't be so disappointed. Let us go and shop for a good pair of shoes and gym wear", Rashv was holding a leaflet in his hand and staring piercingly at it. "Look Mom! They even have a flat 20% discount for the ladies! It's their 20th anniversary you see!" he exclaimed with a sheepish grin on his face.

"Now that's the way it's done!" chuckled his mom as she took the leaflet from his hands and browsed through the deals. They had their dose of caffeine and got up to leave.

They came back from their shopping spree quite late in the evening, holding lots of shopping bags in their hands. As it was getting late and the evening hour at the gym was about to begin, Rashv got ready, gelled his hair and looked at himself into the mirror. "Perfect", he approved of his look and left hurriedly.

He reached the gym just in time and was pleased to see various equipments systematically placed at an equal distance. There was an energetic burst of loud music creating the atmosphere of an urgency to move one's limbs. Rashv had been standing at the entrance looking at the fitness enthusiasts deeply engrossed in a struggle to raise the bar and tone their muscles. But overall he was pretty amused to see them trying their best to prove to themselves that they disliked their God-gifted physique and the shape they were in and were hence trying hard to better it. Even though the argument for this is that maintaining your fitness through exercising is good for health but somewhere down the line, he thought, sweating over the gym equipment becomes only a matter of enhancing one's physical parameters for most people. Moreover, people stop working out once they have reached their goals. Rarely does one aim for an all around improvement in health through a conscious focus on changing unhealthy habits along with physical exercise and switching to a healthier lifestyle. Controlling one's instincts towards food is always tough and a disciplined regime is not everyone's cup of tea. Perhaps he was also trying to reason himself out of his decision to change his physical habits so drastically and so soon, especially when he saw the others huff and puff it out on the machines.

"It looks so hard!"

He had been standing at the entrance evaluating the pros and cons of having taken the gym membership and gathering up the courage to join the others when the gym instructor suddenly nudged him from behind and disturbed his train of thoughts.

"So Mr. Fabulous, let us get moving and start with simple warm-up exercises followed by cardio", the instructor was noticeably amused upon reading the print on his tee which read, "I'm not Fat. I am Fabulous."

Rashv nodded and moved to a large room where they began the warm-ups as per the instructions. He huffed and puffed profusely as he began to move his inert muscles and found his whole body resisting any new moves. His face gleamed in sweat drops and nerve pain took over his entire body. In just a short while, he was completely worn-out and reduced to a soaking bag with his tee dripping with sweat. A few people around even glanced at him and giggled at the way in which he was reduced to a wet potato within a few minutes of exercising.

Looking at his reaction to warm-up exercises, the instructor thought it was fit to call it a day for him and administered a detailed set of printed and verbal instructions about the exercising regime he was supposed to follow from now on and other diet-related instructions, which Rashv was least interested in listening to, mainly owing to his fatigued state of mind and body. Finally, after an hour, he managed to gather up his frittered energy and dragged himself out of the gym towards his home, all the while looking like a fish thrown out of deep waters- out of breath and out of senses!

Rashv crashed on his bed as each of his joints was sore with pain. As advised by the instructor, he lay down on the bed with a hot water bag, soothing his throbbing muscular pain and cursed himself in annoyance for having chosen to join the gym and putting himself through all of this voluntarily. He sipped some water from a bottle to calm the incessant thumping of his heart and limped over towards his mom who was sitting at the study table with a chart and pencil, preparing a broad design for her new assignment.

"What's for dinner, Mom?"

"Your favourite..."

"No, please prepare a normal 'paratha' for me with some

'sabzi' to go with it."

"That's great, Rashv!" exclaimed his mom as he half-heartedly handed over the diet chart to her. A sudden urge of taking physical exercise as a challenge grew over him as he realised that change is good if it is for one's betterment. Perhaps even more than that he had his number game playing at the back of his mind and he realised that he had to start from somewhere to take the course of his life in his own hands. The first step in that direction demanded a complete transformation of his external personality, however tough it may feel at first.

The next evening he took his own sweet time to complete his entire set of prescribed exercises at the gym which included push-ups, skipping, cycling, and stomach toning exercises. Just when he was about to leave, his phone rang up. It was Rahul.

"Hey, what happened to you? You ran off that day as if your ass was on fire."

"I... I..." Rahul stammered.

"What? Come on now and speak up!" Rashv chuckled.

Rahul on the other hand, was still stammering.

"Fine! Call me when you muster enough courage to speak. Don't waste my time." He was just about to hang up the phone when Rahul finally spoke.

"I... I... I experienced... a nightfall dreaming about her." He blurted out at thrice his normal speed of talking.

Rashv was left shell-shocked for a while. At first, he didn't know how to react but then he howled in laughter, clutching his stomach as he descended the flight of stairs, halting at every other step for a breather. He was so engrossed in congratulating Rahul that he could not hear someone from behind asking him to give way. Since he was so lost in his own conversation, Rashv did not pay heed to him and in a hurry, the person happened to rub shoulders with him as he overtook him in a hurry and fled. The space on the stairs was too narrow for two persons to cross at the same time and as a result of the impact of brushing his shoulder with the stranger, Rashv who was almost nearing the end of the stairs was suddenly pushed two steps further down in a jiffy and bammm! He bumped into another person who was about to take a turn to climb the next flight of stairs. Consequently, he pushed her a bit backward. All of this happened in a quick sequence of events and Rashv, in a sudden reaction to this, subconsciously let his right hand out to support her as she delicately rested on his outstretched hand for a fleeting moment and their eyes met before they both lost balance and fell on top of the other.

CHAPTER 13

"What? Will you just stop looking at me like an idiot and help me pick myself up?" she was livid, her face flushed with anger.

Her loud words went unheard as Rashv's eyes kept looking at her red face. He noticed the glistening set of wide eyes, nicely done with a touch of colorful mascara that enhanced the beauty of her eyelashes. The delicate curves of her face along with the slight moistness formed by small sweat drops on her forehead grew on his senses. The flying locks, the fullness of her luscious lips, her strong back and her tall curvy body made Rashv's heartbeats go wild. It was nothing short of a scene taken out of a Bollywood movie. A strong punch at Rashv's stomach brought him back to reality and he took a footstep back. He groaned in slight pain, closed his mouth, and took the support of the side wall.

"Oww!" he grimaced in pain. "I am sorry. Some fool pushed me from behind and I lost my balance."

"You better be sorry", she replied. "By the way", she continued, "It seems like someone is constantly yelling from that device in your hand." She added and started adjusting the sleeveless tee that she was wearing, ran her hand along her wavy curls, and began climbing the stairs.

Rashv took notice that Rahul was on the line and he blurted, 'Call you back soon' at a speed of a nanosecond and disconnected the call. He didn't want to miss savoring this chance encounter. He for once thanked the person who had pushed him at her. He was about to call out to her when she suddenly stopped and turned around to look at Rashv.

"Hi, I am Ambar..." she held out her right hand for a handshake.

"Hiieee!" Rashv replied with an enthusiasm akin to that of a 5-year-old kid as he enthusiastically shook hands with her. The hand shaking thing lasted for more than a while as Rashv kept shaking her hand with his eyes looking directly into hers. Ambar could only smile at this; feeling slightly awkward at Rashv's weird behaviour.

"It seems like he has never seen a girl from so close." She coughed and managed to hide a wicked smile as she pressed her fingers tightly around Rashv's hand. Rashv felt a sharp pain in his wrist bones and immediately released his hand from what seemed like a never-ending handshake.

Ambar gave him a flirty little smile, pushing back the loose strand of her hair that had strayed to her lips and began climbing the stairs.

Rashv's heartbeat accelerated from 0-100 within 5 seconds. No one had ever given him such strong vibes and that too in just a single encounter. His heart did a wild skip as he smiled looking at Ambar's retreating back.

He was on cloud nine for the most part of the evening. "That punch really had some power in it", he thought, sitting across the parapet of his living hall balcony enjoying the coolness of a light. The best of Michael Jackson's songs gave him company on his iPod till hunger pangs began to churn the insides of his stomach.

Rashv had a healthy dinner as recommended by his gym instructor and watched a movie with his mom. He had collapsed into sleep midway into the movie when his mom checked on him. She smiled and switched off the movie player leaving Rashv to sleep with dreams of the day's most memorable moment – meeting Ambar, playing on his mind over and over again.

He spent a major portion of the following day with Rahul and teased him about Rahul's moment of masculinity, Googled about it and had fun at his expense based on the search results. On a serious note, he advised Rahul to take it easy and plan out things well.

Evening came and Rashv made the customary check-in at the state of the art gym he had religiously been attending for a week now, without any fail. His eyes kept on looking out for Amber and he silently hoped for another meeting with her. However, for a majority of his time there, he didn't get an opportunity to meet her. He exercised slowly, checking out the entrance after every little while, expecting Ambar to walk in anytime. Rashv was almost at the end of his daily exercise regime when Ambar made a silent entrance. He noticed her from a corner of his eye and immediately put his head down trying to give the impression of being totally engrossed in his workout, looking at the instruction manual on the treadmill. He wanted to see whether Ambar would notice him or it was just a one-off event that day. Rashv's heartbeat zoomed off to the sky as he noticed Ambar walk towards him. He was by now slightly breathless due to increasing speed on the treadmill. Unable to catch his breath, he fumbled on the treadmill, and as a result, he couldn't keep pace with the speeding treadmill and almost got off balance. He was about to fall when Ambar lent him her helping hand.

"Easy, easy, Rashv!", she smirked as Rashv took her support so as to avoid hitting the floor with a loud thud and probably cause some cracks in the flooring. Rashv bit his tongue as he flushed and tried to calm down. He managed to balance himself after a moment or two and stood back on his feet.

"Thanks, Ambar. It seems like we have completed a full circle with this!" he smiled.

"Indeed we may have", she replied haughtily and walked away to begin her exercises. Rashv merely stood there observing her walk away from him. Her hair was neatly tied into a ponytail. From whatever little time they had spent together, Rashv sensed that Ambar was only being friendly with him and it made him slightly disappointed as she did not stop to have a proper conversation with him even though she remembered him from that day which gave him a slight consolation.

With just a few days left for the college to commence its final year lectures, Rashv was still undecided about continuing with the coaching classes. Not because of the particular incident with Beenal but somewhere he felt that studying on his own would be good for him just like it had been all these years.

The next couple of days he slept like there was no end to it, waking up only to make his stomach happy and to visit the gym. But on the other hand, he had also started exercising diligently, as per the workout plan designed for him. He visited the gym at his usual timing i.e., in the evening but Ambar was nowhere to be seen for several days. It was the first time in many years that he had become conscious about transforming from fat to fit, and his personal scheme of things was his constant guiding force.

Chapter 14

The first day of the last year at college was full of exuberance. The students were seen exchanging smiles, high fives and hugs. He noticed that everyone in the campus was happy meeting their friends after so many days. Although most of them had been regularly meeting up either at coaching classes or for some evening fun, they were happy to be back at the place from where their careers would be etched.

It was a long solitary walk for Rashv as he kept on looking at the swarm of students leaning upon each other, resting their heads and sharing a carefree moment. He replied with a smile to all those who greeted him and acknowledged his presence. It felt as though he was a stranger in a known place. A slight sting of his friendship gone sour with Heta was still there in his heart. But bygones were bygones now. If he were to meet her now, he was sure that they would be fine, more or less. Anyway, it all did not matter so much anymore; he reminded himself.

The class was moderately full. It being the first day, most of the students took to have a leisurely time at the college canteen or strolled around the college premises. In other words, they blatantly bunked the lectures. Whereas on the other hand, the only company Rashv had was that of his best friend Rahul who also seemed least interested in the lecture. He was busy chatting away on his phone with a series of messages being exchanged between him and his new girlfriend. As a result, Rashv was left to be all ears to what the various professors had to say apart from one, the economics professor whom Rashv detested from day one for some unknown reasons. Probably it was because of his old school style of teaching which focused on rote learning which made the students lose interest in the subject. This was also true in general for the other teachers in the college. When it gets tough to associate meaning to your subject, it becomes a dull burden which one bears without any choice.

Rashv came back home with a dizzy head and a famished self. He took a bowl of salad kept by his mom in the refrigerator along with slices of apples and a banana to satiate his hunger pangs. It was pretty evident that he had begun to take his diet and exercises very seriously. Since the past few days, he desperately waited for the evening to hit the gym.

One day, he started off with basic exercises and then took to more serious fat burning and muscle enhancing exercises. He did gasp for breath in between the exercises but with every exercise, he tested his endurance and was pretty happy with the result. He completed his day at the gym with a bit of cardio and was ready to leave. Just as he was exiting from the gym he again bumped into Ambar although not literally this time. He had showered and changed and had applied the mantastic deodorant onto his tee and left his hair disheveled with drops of water dripping down from his head.

"Did you just empty the water tank onto your head and splash the entire woody fragrance from the Deo bottle onto your tee?" Ambar asked.

"Where did the customary greetings go?"

"They got scared seeing the "Fabulous" Rashv in this avatar. They are used to seeing a huffing and puffing Rashv, you see!" she chuckled and greeted Rashv with a wave of her fingers.

They stood there for some time in an awkward silence, both of them avoiding each other's gaze, looking sideways.

"I think I need to leave now" Rashv broke the silence and moved aside towards the stairways away from Ambar's sight.

"Rashv, wait a minute. I hope you won't mind exchanging your number with me", she enquired.

"Of course, I wouldn't", he replied and they exchanged

numbers.

A mischievous smile broke across Ambar's face as she waved goodbye to Rashv, and on the other hand, Rashv was smiling too, thinking only about his game of fate.

He jumped and punched in the air and walked away, plugging in his earphones and enjoying the music. He didn't intend to take things at a super fast pace. Instead, he wanted to play the wait-and-watch-game this time by not coming off as too obvious to Ambar that he wanted to date her.

On the other hand, Ambar too made it a point not to come across Rashv as often but once in a while initially and thought of pitching it up later depending on how it went with him.

There were one-off days in between when a simple 'Hello' and 'Wassup' would occupy his Whatsapp which would then follow with a series of messages exchanged with Ambar ranging from personal issues like how parents can get extremely unreasonable at times to the fashion trends one can follow.

"Orange is the new black."

"Is it?"

"Yes, but you need to carry it off well else you will be ridiculed. Also, eye-catching slogans on Tees are 'in' which can be paired with a jacket or a shrug either matching or in contrast to the tee whichever suits you well", pinged Rashv in a series of WhatsApp messages to Ambar.

"Hmm... you seem to be pretty high on fashion knowledge huh, Mr. Fabulous?"

"Aah... that's just one of my favourite pass times", he replied with a smiley.

The unending chats sometimes went on for hours and ended on an emotional high. They had begun to exchange their 'Good night and Sweet dreams' almost on a daily basis now.

THE 23RD GIRL

The following evening Rashv was in the gym toning his chest. A strict diet regime had helped Rashv to go that extra mile without huffing and puffing so much. The trainer would assist him whenever needed and was pretty impressed with the progress that he showed although it was barely a few weeks that he had begun with the exercises. The gym was cramped for space as a majority of its patrons thronged the gym in the evening hours when all the working people and college students head to the gym; some for pure exercising, some for free Wi-Fi and some only to spend their time chatting with fellow patrons turned friends.

Rashv was deeply engrossed in exercising, shifting from one equipment to another. The gym was full of people and so the queue to use the machines was increasing with time. Rashv didn't let the claustrophobic environment stop him from using the different types of equipment. He had not allowed himself to become complacent these days so he resisted his feelings of dislike and frustration and patiently waited for his turn to use the machines along with a couple of other people, forced to inhale the stuffy air without making any fuss. And in an attempt to grab the equipment as quickly as possible, he inadvertently shoved aside one of the patrons waiting for the equipment to be vacant, thereby leading to a loud exchange of words which looked like it could culminate into a brawl anytime. A timely intervention from Ambar, who was present there, subsided the argument. But there was an unnecessary fallout from the event. The guy Rashv had been fighting with, challenged him for a push-ups match on the weekend and it was declared that the winner would be allowed to use the machines first if the two of them happened to be at the gym at the same time for the rest of their gym membership. Ambar took Rashv out of the gym, sacrificing her exercises for him and tried to cool him down. She looked frantically on the either sides of the road, pacing up every second.

"What are you waiting for?" Rashv asked looking at her

searching eyes, after walking with her silently for a whole five minutes.

"Ice", she replied and continued. "You need to cool down, Rashv. What was that unnecessary mess that you created over there? Was it necessary to get into a public brawl? And what would you do if you lose? That guy over there is far better built up than you. Did you realise that when you made that stupid bet or had you gone all senseless? In my opinion, what you did was extremely uncalled for and you will end up losing. It was actually very foolish of you. I did not expect this from you at all!" she sounded exasperated.

Rashv was surprised that Ambar did not support him. In fact, he was disappointed that she thought less of him. He looked at her for a moment and smiled. In all the drama that had happened over the past few minutes, he realised that he had not taken proper notice of her. It was her usual, familiar face... but she looked a bit different. As he looked more closely, he realised that she seemed to have got a nice hair cut with her hair streaked in wine coloured highlights. It streamed over her temples and fell across her white shoulders. A pair of silver danglers hung nicely from her ears and a delicate little neck piece added to the overall simple and minimalistic look. She had not changed from her workout clothes and he noticed that the light blue tank top running deep at her back teamed with a black Capri gave her a perfect contemporary yet classy look that seemed to suit her very much.

"It's the second time that you are left open-mouthed, Mr. Awesome!" Ambar shook Rashv from his trance as she realised that he had been staring at her for over a minute.

"That new haircut and highlights look awesome on you!"

"Thanks for changing the topic. It only means that you really don't care about what I have been talking about!" she sounded irritated to the core. "And I have to leave now. I think you are mature enough to choose and handle your battles with ease. We got a glimpse of that a short while ago at the gym", she picked up her bag and unclipped her hair which was held in a high bun. Her soft tresses fell like a cascade on her shoulders and framed her face. All this time Rashv had been looking at her, stupefied. There is something wildly attractive about certain things that women do. Ambar had been constantly playing with her tresses, rolling them between her fingers, tossing them from one side to the other, showing off her toned back. Rashv, on the other hand, was finding it hard to recover from the attraction. There was a strange silence between the two now, thick with anticipation. The mood was definitely uncomfortable. They walked out together with not a single word being exchanged between them. They were about to reach home when Rashv broke the silence.

"Ambar, I know that you do not approve of what happened in the gym today. But I hope you would be there for me when the match happens this weekend."

"Of course, I will be there. Who would save you if you get into another mess, Mr. Fabulous" There was a hint of sarcasm in her voice as she smiled and they both turned towards their respective houses.

"Bye! See you tomorrow!"

Rashv was a nervous wreck for the most part of the evening. Till some time back it was Ambar who had doubted his ability to ace a push-ups contest and now he himself began to have second thoughts on the incident, thinking of how knee-jerk his reaction had been and whether he could have reacted in a different way. Reflecting on the incident, it became doubly clear to him that he accepted the challenge only because of the way in which the guy had hurt his ego. After all, it seemed to be the only thing he could have done at the spur of that moment, given that the guy had publically challenged him in front of the whole crowd of people and foolish or not, he could not refuse the challenge as he feared that it would seem as if he had chickened out of fear. It was unacceptable!

Just then his eyes fell on the shelf. The sight of the red box on the shelf made him cringe as he recollected the incident or rather the series of incidents with Beenal and his resultant decision regarding the game of fate. It had been a fairly recent incident and he was not willing to have another insulting experience anytime soon. The next few days he spent training hard at the gym, preparing for the match and trying to do intensive exercises to improve his stamina followed up with a practice session of push-ups. During most of his time at the gym, Ambar was there beside him, urging and encouraging him for putting in that little bit of extra effort.

"Rashv? I am very concerned about you. You are not making good progress! This is not the way you can win that bet. There's still time. I would suggest you go and speak to that guy over there and tell him that it did not actually mean anything at all and that you would not participate in that stupid challenge." She tried to reason with him after they had completed their exercises and were about to leave.

"No way, Ambar! Not at all! There's no way I can pull out like that at this stage. I would end up looking gutless. Do you want me to be laughed at? Is that what you want? I don't know how I will fare against him but I certainly cannot give up thinking that I might fail. I am not as frail as you think, Ambar. I would not give up." Rashv seemed to have made up his mind.

Ambar raised her brow and gave him a prodding look. She could not decide as to whether he was being foolhardy or if his courage really amounted to anything at all.

"Okay then. Go on. I'm there", she sounded resigned. "I need to go now. I've got something important to catch up at home", she said cutting the moment abruptly and started walking away.

Rashv stood there for a moment and then began to follow her.

Before Rashv could utter any word, Ambar turned around and came closer to him.

"See you tomorrow for your push-ups match, Mr. Fabulous", Ambar said in a thick voice, patted his cheeks, hailed a taxi and zoomed off.

CHAPTER 15

Ambar rolled down the window of the taxi and took in the cool evening breeze. The air felt like a soft cool breeze on her sassy face and carelessly tousled her soft feminine curls. It was a beautiful weather indeed.

"Everything is going right on track", she thought. For once she even doubted herself whether whatever she was doing was correct. She tried to be calm and composed while travelling down the rutted lane of feelings and emotions. Her heart didn't allow her to continue playing with Rashv's feelings. "Poor Rashv", she sympathized. But sometimes the line between correct and incorrect fades and you have to do things which might not be good in nature but good for your heart at the end of the day.

She perched herself upon one of the benches on the promenade facing the sea. This was her favourite spot in the entire city. She often came here to sit in silence when her mind was a wreck, full of conflicting thoughts. She saw the sun setting down far away, dipping into the horizon.

Rashv knew little of what was likely to approach him in near future. On the other hand, Ambar was excited thinking of how she was inching closer to her scheme of things irrespective of whether Rashv would win the push-ups match or not.

Back at the gym, Rashv was getting all geared up for the match by warming up and flexing his now slightly evident muscles. He was for a moment undecided on what jersey to wear, the one bearing the number 23 or without it. Even though he was pretty superstitious about the number, since he was wearing one of those t-shirts not bearing the number on the day when he had agreed to the push-ups match, he decided to go with the jersey without bearing number 23 on it.

"I know you are now beginning to be man enough to handle

your battles and accept challenges but at least you could have informed me about it? We visit the same gym but at different times in case you have forgotten", chided his mom.

"I thought you would not like me getting into such fights."

"Well, that is for you to decide whether it is good for you or not. All I am interested in is that you should have informed me. It is your battle which you have gladly accepted, so go ahead. I am not going to be there with you to advice on your decisions every time." His mom gave a curt reply to Rashv.

"Mom, please. Stop it. This is not the time for you to bicker."

"Oh yes! Today's generation! If you say a line or two more, they find it irritating!"

Rashv eyed his mom as she stood before him, almost teary eyed.

"Ok. Calm down", he got up and took her face in his hands, wiping away the tears.

"I will be fine, mom!", he assured her.

"Okay, take care of yourself, Rashv! "She waved her hand as Rashv left for the gym hurriedly.

Rashv stood at the entrance door, amazed at what he saw. The gym had been transformed into a party hall. All sorts of cheery faces welcomed him, pointing fingers, indicating that one of the challengers had arrived. "Wasn't the challenge a bit on a personal side which could have been done without as much fanfare? I never thought that it was such a big deal. Or has someone made it into a big deal?" He mused as he stood there.

Rashv inhaled deeply and entered inside the gym. A round of claps greeted him as soon as he entered. "Seems like it is going to be way bigger than I had ever imagined this challenge to be", he was feeling concerned now. He acknowledged their cheer with a nod of his head but did he really have a choice? He could recognize a few known faces, standing and waiting eagerly for the match to commence, though he had never interacted with them. There was no excitement visible on his face as if he already knew the reason behind the trumpet blast that was on display inside the gym. Somebody has planned this out for sure. 'Who could it possibly be', he wondered. 'What if I lose?' His confidence was shaking already. He was nervously looking out for the guy who had challenged him. Meanwhile, Ambar was nowhere to be seen. He placed his bag aside in one of the corners and started warming up. He took to the exercising machines without caring to participate in the fuss.

"Hey, buddy! What's going on?" It was J, his competitor. He reached over to Rashv and patted on his back. J. That's what everyone used to call him at the gym.

"J for Jerk!" Rashv thought.

"I hope you are not scared of what I have achieved in just a couple of months", Rashv smiled as he flexed his muscles. It was nothing more than a slight bulging shape on his biceps but even that was a lot for Rashv who had seen fat mount on his body all these years.

J roared out laughing. "Do I need to be scared of you? Really! Haven't you seen your bean bag abs?" he jibed.

Rashv eyed him as piercingly as he could and left as soon as he caught a sight of his only supporter – Ambar.

She patted on his shoulder from behind. "All set, Mr. Fabulous?" Ambar raised her brow and smiled.

Rashv smiled and nodded. The environment was electric with music beating at a high volume. Ambar was looking pretty even in her simple hooded full sleeved tee and a printed legging. Just then an announcement was made for the challenge to commence. The voice also announced that as it was also the owner's birthday, a friendly challenge from the other patrons was invited and the winners would be graced with hampers and coupons. That's when Rashv realised the reason behind all the decoration. The music stopped playing as rounds of claps and whistles took its place with voices cheering for both of them. J first took the center most area of the gym and settled himself in a stretched position, waiting for the start signal. They had decided that the one who would complete the maximum number of push-ups in a minute would win the competition.

J started the push-ups as swiftly as he could. Everyone present there surrounded him forming a circle and kept counting the push-ups with a roar. J was laboriously pushing himself and let out a grunt with each push-up. He tried to push himself further but his stamina gave up after completing 20 push-ups in fifty seconds. A difficult feat indeed!

It was Rashv's turn and he needed a minimum of 21 complete push-ups in less than fifty seconds to win. Rashv started slowly, taking his own time with Ambar continuously cheering for him, encouraging him with her constant motivational talk. Among all the people present, she was the only one cheering on loudly for him. Rashv, on the other hand, seemed to be in no hurry to complete more than 21 push-ups in less than fifty seconds. The way in which he had started gave a clear indication that he was not going to win. "This is no contest at all", screamed someone from behind and the voice fell on Ambar's ears. But she still kept on cheering for him. Towards the end, Ambar was the only one continuing to cheer and motivate him. The spectators seemed to lose all interest in his non-competitive performance and they started mocking Rashv and Ambar. Some even went back to the machines and began their routines. J stood all smiles as he kept on pointing at the watch. But Rashv continued till his heart, mind and body allowed him. He took his own sweet little time to complete the challenge, managing to do a paltry total of fifteen push-ups in around six minutes and as such, he clearly lost the challenge.

THE 23RD GIRL

Rashv relaxed himself with a hot water shower inside the locker room and changed into a yellow Tantra tee which read "Fate and I are at loggerheads" and a totally contrast white track pant. He smiled that Ambar was upset at his loss and was frowning as J was being awarded a bowl of fresh salad and a shopping voucher in celebration of his victory and the owner's birthday.

"Congratulations!" Rashv uttered meekly as he managed a small smile and shook hands with J.

"I think you would always remember this day. It would have been good for you had you sized yourself up before accepting a challenge with me." J smirked at him.

Rashv simply nodded and set off from the gym, much to Ambar's embarrassment. The friendly matches continued between various other members as it was celebration time.

"I thought you would be a bit dejected after losing the challenge", Ambar's face had turned red with anger as they left the gym.

"Why would I be dejected?" replied Rashv and continued. "What did you think, that I would agree for a challenge just to lose? No dear. I was actually competing with myself and not with that Jack of a person. I was testing my stamina which was zero at the start and is improving now. From fat to fit, if I may say so, I have traveled a fair amount of distance for my health and well-being. And also thanks to you for not even once being pessimistic for me and for the way you cheered for me throughout", Rashv replied.

Ambar gave him a measured smile as her mind started to prick her again. She ignored it for a while but all of a sudden she clasped Rashv's hand, sliding her fingers into his so as to divert her mind.

A wave of electric current rushed all through Rashv's body as he halted in his way and quivered slightly. Ambar clutched his hand tightly and came too close for Rashv's comfort.

"A cup of hot coffee and your 'Fabulous' company is what I have been craving for. What say, Rashv?" She murmured in a husky seductive voice and gave him a swooning smile as she created some space between them and started taking smaller steps ahead of him.

Rashv followed her, grabbed her hand, and turned her around as her eyes met his. He pulled her a bit closer as his senses were wrecked with the sweet cologne that she was wearing. He flicked a loose strand of her hair and murmured in her ear, "This Sunday afternoon at Barista near JP flyover." But before she could react, Rashv walked away towards his home. Ambar stood there completely dumbstruck as she had not expected Rashv to run away and secondly she couldn't believe that he had agreed for a cup of coffee but on a Sunday and not now. Probably Rashv was feeling a bit awkward to go on a date with her, she thought. She could not help but smile when she recalled how she could hear Rashv's breathing when he came close to her. It gave her tingles.

Rashv had never ever expected that he would come so freaking close to her in reality. And it was only because Ambar was suddenly showing a growing interest in him. His cautious brain at first didn't allow his heart to slip away and agree on the impromptu date that she had asked for. It acted wisely to keep his heart under control and not allow it to be easily hassled by her charms. Though Rashv was eager to date Ambar and bring to his shelf some form of gift that could act as a souvenir to further his game of fate, he didn't do so. Instead, he listened to his brain's advice and took a few days time so as to avoid coming off as desperate, having readily agreed to a date.

Sunday came with an early morning call from Ambar; as if the constant exchange of messages in the past few days on Whatsapp weren't enough.

"Don't you think your duvet requires you more than anyone else right now at this ungodly hour?" Rashv avoided the customary 'Hello'.

"Thinking about meeting you over a cup of coffee is getting the better of me I guess!" Ambar replied in a thick voice with a sleepy undertone.

Rashv tried hard to curb his happiness as he realised that Ambar was desperate to go on a date with him. He smiled wickedly as he felt like he was now another step closer towards his goal. Ambar, on the other end, was controlling her laughter, as she constantly tried to suggest that she was longing to meet him. Though there was some percentage of truth in whatever she said to Rashv but majority of what she was saying was for a particular purpose and reason.

They ended the call after almost an hour and both of them were pleased with how well their respective plans were working out.

Soon, it was time for the date. Rashv tried not to dress too differently from what he usually wore. He did not want her to assume that he was too happy to turn up for the date. "Some things are better left unchanged, for instance, your appearance and then too especially when you look so perfect", he smiled at the mirror. Rashv's mom was busy in the kitchen. He somehow managed to slip out unseen. "Thanks for the help, God", he looked upwards and heaved a sigh of relief as now he would not have to answer a string of queries from his mother. Just like how it is with a lot of mommy's boys, he found it very tough to lie to his mom.

Rashv reached the destination twenty minutes early and took the table placed exactly in the center. The coffee shop was packed with teenagers and young adults, it being a Sunday afternoon. Rashv kept looking at his phone and at the entrance. He was eagerly waiting for Ambar.

"How ironic it is that people going on a date are usually happy thinking about their future with regards to their relationship whereas here I am partly happy for being on my first date ever and partly sad that I'll have to kill this relationship and move on", he mused waiting for Ambar to arrive.

"Thinking about me, Mr. Fabulous?" Ambar was visibly happy.

"Hey, Ambar! Please have a seat" Rashv pulled a chair for her. "And you are looking so pretty today!" he paid her a sincere compliment.

"Don't flatter me, Rashv. I am simply wearing a collared tee and jeans."

"Did I say anything about your clothes?" Rashv raised his brow with a grin on his face. Ambar was left flushed for few seconds.

"Ambar will you please stop blushing. It's getting hard for me over here" he said, matter of factly, as he placed his fingers on the tissue paper that she was fidgeting with.

She gave him a swooning smile.

"Am I sitting in front of the latest edition of a fashion magazine?" Ambar teased.

"No, you are sitting in front of the editor of the latest edition of a fashion magazine", Rashv responded with a wink.

"Ahh... that was very witty of you, Mr. Fabulous", she smiled and looked directly into Rashv's eyes as they chatted and laughed for hours before they decided to leave the coffee shop and spend the evening along the beach side.

A curious and a jealous pair of eyes were keeping a watch on Ambar and her activities. Ambar being completely aware ignored it purposefully. They left the cafe, hands clasped together tightly, completely lost in each other, or so it seemed to the others.

CHAPTER 16

The wooden bench at the promenade facing the sea was a bit warm from the day's heat. A slight nip in the air gave them some much-needed respite from the humidity. There was a fair amount of distance between them as they sat watching the tides rise and fall. They had been incessantly talking to each other for the past few hours. It looked like a good date. The yellow of the sun had yielded to an orange shade that splattered a beautiful hue across the horizon.

"It's so beautiful, isn't it?" Ambar pointed at the horizon with such a childlike glee that it caught Rashv's attention, bringing him back from his thoughts that were all focused on his game.

He looked at her with a very focused look on his face.

"It feels like I am in seventh heaven" Ambar marveled at nature's beauty as she stared at the sky.

"Some things are just way too beautiful to be captured in a picture. They can only be felt and lived", Rashv replied looking towards Ambar with tender eyes as he put the stray lock of hair around her cheek behind her ear. She flushed as Rashv's hand brushed her cheek as she allowed him to put the stray lock of hair in place. Both of them had now come close to each other. They could hear each other's heart beating heavily and were just inches away from their first kiss. They stood momentarily gazing into each other's eyes, with love blooming between them but inside both of them knew what exactly they both were up to. And then suddenly, sanity prevailed as Rashv moved back, although biting his lower lip in rising excitement of getting to kiss someone for the first time.

A stranger had been keeping an eye on all that was taking place between Ambar and Rashv from behind the branches of nearby trees.

Being conscious of his game and needing some souvenir for the same, Rashv proposed, biting his own words, "Well, there are some beautiful memories which still can be easily captured, felt and lived", he took out his phone and took a selfie as he kissed her cheek. They posed for a couple of clicks, one with the lavender-pink sky as the background and another with the sea.

Ambar suggested that they take a stroll on the beach and Rashv agreed. They enjoyed the coolness of the sand on their bare feet, the sound of the waves lapping on the shores, the chirping of the birds and the sweet smell of the salty water mixed with sand which together made for a very pleasant evening. The cool wet breeze swirled around them and both of them lost all track of time.

They engaged in some hearty banter as they strolled, walking hand in hand, flicking the sand particles by their feet and splashing the sea water. They giggled through their way playing, sometimes balancing on each other's shoulders, and sometimes holding onto the other by their waist. For a moment he wondered if she could have noticed the game that he was playing. But Rashv decided not to think too much as Ambar seemed to be in a jovial mood. Still somewhere deep inside his heart, there was a buildup of insecurity and thoughts of what would actually happen if she came to know.

At the same time, the eager eye kept following them secretly, keeping a fair amount of distance to avoid being noticed.

After being completely exhausted from the soul-satisfying walk-play that went on for what appeared like an eternity, they decided to sit on the cool sand and enjoy the last rays of the setting sun. Rashv stretched his legs out facing the sea and rested himself with the support of his hands stretched backward. Ambar sat with an upright back. They were so lost in their joie de vivre that they didn't realise that it was beginning to turn dark. Or maybe it was simply a chance to be in the moment and enjoy the feeling while it lasted.

At that juncture, Ambar decided to begin with her scheme of things and prayed that everything went according to her plan with some help from the almighty. She opened her bag, and gave a box of Lindt Dark Chocolates as a gift to Rashv.

At first, he refused to accept them but with some consistent pleading on her part, Rashv agreed and accepted the box.

"Thank you so much for making this date so special and now chocolaty, Amber", he winked as he realised that he had inched a step closer towards his game but in a way that it had not become evident to Ambar.

"My pleasure, it was such an exciting time to be alongside you and share some beautiful moments. Thank you for being such a wonderful company and making this date so memorable. You are truly an amazing person", she replied without looking up and meeting his eyes.

"It's time for some action", the stranger spying over them mumbled and quickly walked over to where they were seated.

Although it was almost dark, Ambar felt a shadow reaching up from behind them. Initially, she brushed it off as a figment of her imagination but later she was sure of who it was as she could sense a familiar air around, air that reeked of unfaithfulness which was of low human quality.

Within no time, the stranger grabbed Rashv from behind, pulled him by his collar, turned him around and landed a punch straight into his stomach. Rashv's mind simply could not understand what was happening as he limped in pain, clutching his stomach tightly. If that wasn't enough, he landed another blow which hit Rashv exactly on his forehead. That was enough for Rashv to land flat on his back with a blurring vision that made him unable to identify the face.

"So YOU will give her a wonderful company? YOU will hold

her hand and come close to kissing her? YOU?" he burst out and gave another kick to Rashv. Once, Twice, Thrice! Rashv moaned in deep pain and just then Ambar grabbed the figure from behind and emptied half a can of pepper spray onto his face and eyes which made him crumble in pain, coughing heavily, as he sat rubbing his eyes.

"You got what you deserve, Mr. Anjan", Ambar fumed and sprayed some more from the can. "What did you think? I would not realise that you had been two-timing me? Now you will realise how much it hurts when your loyal girlfriend backstabs you and 'enjoys' her time with someone else. You were by my side because I am rich and so that you can flaunt me among your friends, isn't it? But I am sorry it won't happen anymore." Ambar kicked Anjan around his groin not once but twice which was enough for him to pass out in pain.

Ambar thanked the almighty for helping her succeed in her mission and felt sorry for having to turn a dark shade of grey for Rashv. "But sometimes you have to mould yourself according to situations and not fret whether it was right or wrong", she tried to calm her restless mind. She looked around to check if anyone else had witnessed the happenings but luckily no one was around. She apologised to Rashv with a run of her fingers in his hair, somehow lifted him up, wrapped one of his arms around her shoulders and dragged him towards a bench.

She then dialed a number, blurted out something and looked over to the promenade. It looked like she was waiting for someone. And within minutes, a chauffeur emerged from a car parked outside and waved towards her. She raised her hand and gestured at him, asking him to wait. Ambar stooped over Rashv, who was possibly still unconscious, placed an envelope into his hand, and patted on his right cheek in an attempt to bring him back to his senses. She stood there looking at him for a while and in a sudden surge of emotions pushed herself closer to Rashv's face and kissed his grainy and salty lips without any fuss, thus setting fire to Rashv's unconscious state and bringing him back to consciousness. Rashv simply went with the flow and pulled her a bit closer to him as he kissed her with equal gusto if not more and matched her moves tongue to tongue, lips with lips.

Though the kiss lasted for not more than a couple of minutes there was something in that kiss, in that budding relation, in that short span of time spent together that left him asking for more but Ambar decided against it and pulled away from him. She apologised for all the mess she had created. She told him that she did not want to give any meaning to a relationship which was started with the basic aim of carrying out a personal vendetta and taking a revenge in which he was used as a scapegoat, although she also admitted to him that she had started liking him. All Rashv could do in that moment was to stare at the sky helplessly and wonder as to what happened to him so suddenly. He was still to come to terms with the fact that he had made a complete fool of himself, yet again. His number game had landed him with another embarrassing episode to make sense of. And in utter dismay, he kicked Anjan while limping towards the exit to fetch an auto. At this point, his heart was all weepy and simpering. He, however, also had a coy smile on his face as he ran his fingers over his lips remembering his first kiss ever.

·

Chapter 17

Rahul laughed his heart out rolling on the floor as Rashv narrated the day's incident in elaborate detail and sulked. He controlled his laughter for a moment as he felt bad for Rashv but soon gave up with a fresh bout of laughter. "Ya ya, laugh at your friend's adversity", Rashv was visibly agitated and threw a pillow at his face. He was in so much pain that it was getting difficult for him to breathe properly. His heart was shattered and torn into pieces with his morale at an all time low. He tried hard to distract his mind from the pain that he was going through but his eyes had already started turning moist.

"It's going to be difficult to forget the past, especially when you both were turning into good friends, shared a kiss too and then suddenly you found yourself unceremoniously pushed out for someone else's mistake. But don't let this incident affect your morale", it was his brain that came forward to his rescue. Rashv gained some control over his emotions. He recollected about the chocolate box and the envelope which Ambar had given him. He opened the envelope to find a hand written sorry card with a smiley drawn at the end. "What the heck? Life is making a complete mockery of me. I mean in the whole wide world she found and chose me to be a scapegoat for her revenge tactics!" he screeched.

"Life's not about how hard of a hit you can give back, it's about how many hits you can take and still keep moving forward", snarled Rahul in a hoarse voice. Rashv smiled at him as he tried to come to terms with what had happened. But what irked him the most at this time was the blow hot and blow cold behaviour of the number 23. He felt a bit perplexed this time and failed to come to any conclusion. The moot question now was whether his decision to ace the number was leading him anywhere and if it really meant anything more than blindly following his personal whims and obsessions.

Months passed and his wounds got covered with scar tissue, lessening his emotional pain. Rashv changed his focus and concentrated on his studies, attending college and trying hard to get fitter and slimmer by visiting the gym daily. The wounds of the past were slowly forgotten and relegated into the recesses of his mind and the letter was placed on his shelf as a souvenir from Ambar.

On the other hand, the activities in the college got bigger day by day as the annual college fest was about to commence in a few weeks. The college premises became a melting pot of youthful energy. From finding volunteers, participants and experts to planning and executing it to perfection, the students were involved in the event to a great extent. A few of the students willingly chose to participate in the three-day event whereas a few others were forced to participate with Rashv happening to fall into the latter category.

"What the hell?" Rashv exclaimed upon receiving an email from the college id. "Dance competition? And Avantika! Paired with ME! What kind of sorcery is this, God? I don't even know the basics of dance; forget thinking of taking part in some dance competition. They cannot just plan an event without considering who can do what." He was determined to meet up with the student body and demand a cancellation of this mismatched pairing.

Rashv stormed through the college corridors as he looked out for the student body representatives. As he passed through the hallway in front of the college auditorium, he stopped outside to gauge the kind of preparations that were going on. A few students were at ease moving to the beats while a few others looked puzzled and forced through the motions, clearly marking out the involuntary participants of the lot.

"God, I can't bear to be a laughing stock, once again. And this time, in front of my entire college." He met up with the cultural committee members and tried to reason with them but to no avail. It was the theme of the year. The best dancers were paired with the novices in a fresh new twist to the usual way in which the annual dance fest was carried out every year. He finally resigned and gave up protesting as all his efforts failed. He left the auditorium, all disappointed and not knowing what to expect next.

CHAPTER 18

"Will I get to learn dance or will she forget dancing?" Rashv smiled as he made his way through the auditorium looking for Avantika where dance practice and rehearsals were taking place.

He was keenly observing the happenings on the stage when he suddenly found himself being twirled around in quick circles and was then left to balance himself with as much suddenness as it came.

"Hi! I'm Avantika. I guess you came here looking for me!" she winked and smiled a full moon grabbing Rashv's hand just when he was about to trip and their eyes met.

She was slimmer than a peeled onion with her hair neatly pulled back into a bun, her figure hugging top accentuating her curves and her long slim legs in suntan tights could have been a sight even for a blind man.

"God has definitely answered my unsaid prayer by presenting an enchanting beauty in front of my eyes", Rashv tried to flirt with her.

Avantika cringed at his cheesy words as she loosened her hold on Rashv's hand momentarily and held it back when he was just inches before hitting the floor. "You flirt with me, you flirt with danger. Consider this as a warning", she croaked and pulled him back.

Rashv got back on his feet and raised both his hands signaling that he got the message and guiltily introduced himself looking at his feet.

She chuckled at his innocent reaction and introduced herself as she made him put on his dancing shoes after doing some cursory warm-up exercises. Avantika made sure that Rashv matched her steps as they were to perform on a Bollywood number. As a result, by the end of the day, his feet had turned sore and he realised that dancing was a mean feat in itself. He had made no progress and ended up frustrating both himself and his dance partner.

"How on the earth are you going to match my steps?" Avantika grumbled as Rashv was completely out of sync with the beats even after practicing for several days. She found him too slow to match her steps as she along with the much-experienced choreographer struggled to make his body move with the beats. After continuously practicing for long hours with both of them totally focussing on Rashv and trying to make him move, they succeeded somewhat as Rashv could finally give them a perfect and a delicate move of his arms and legs in sync with the beat, after practicing one set of moves over several days.

"Bravo!" Avantika clapped excitedly and rushed towards him. She held him by his hand while placing his other hand on her waist as they started swaying to the tunes. Rashv was caught by surprise and didn't even blink an eyelid as his eyes were fixated on hers. He noticed how delicately her face changed expressions as they swayed to and fro, perfecting the step.

"Shall I put some cubes of ice into your tea, in case you have changed your mind?" She tapped him on his shoulders, bringing Rashv back into his proper senses.

"Uh oh... Sorry! Actually, I was thinking that we need to practice some more so that I can get used to your pace, catch the beat and move in a rhythm", he managed to blurt out. He secretly hoped to spend as much time with her as possible. The incident with Ambar had made him more focused and determined and he was not willing to be in a vulnerable position again and get dumped, that too so soon.

"Well, you are right but it's not WE but YOU who need to practice. Also, good that you now realise that it's a couple dance and you need to move in rhythm with me.", she chuckled.

For the entire session that day, Rashv practiced hard but he kept forgetting the steps. "Where is your focus, Rashv?" she took him aside from the stage where they were practicing. "The choreographer is getting worked up and I guess you don't want to be the reason for her hyperventilating, do you?"

"Whoa! I never said that I wanted to be here in the first place. I am trying hard, giving my cent percent. Can't you people see? For you, it all may be easy but for me all of this is not at all easy especially when I am a non-dancer and this is something nobody over here understands or is willing to accept it seems!" there was a slight irritation evident in his tone. With those words, he stormed out of the auditorium.

This sudden burst of anger from Rashv concerned Avantika. She followed him after taking permission from the choreographer. It took her a while to find Rashv who had almost reached outside the college main gate looking for an auto.

"Rashv! Stop!" Avantika held his hand coming from behind, gasping for breath. "What's the matter?" she prodded him. Rashv simply stared at her with a stoic expression and a raised brow.

"What was all that? What happened?"

"Nothing", he replied with a tinge of a smile appearing on his face.

"And now you are smiling and acting all weird" Avantika was livid now as Rashv kept looking out for an auto.

"I don't know as to why you people can't have patience with me. I have never been a dancer."

"Okay, let it be. We'll try again tomorrow. Can you drop me at my apartment before you go back home?" She had given up. They hired an auto and left for home. Rashv was silent throughout. Avantika tried to cheer him up with her small talk. She had forgotten to change from her attire of shorts and vest. "My my... Rashv is getting uncomfortable seeing me in 'such' clothes?" she teased him and playfully pulled his cheeks. Rashv continued to be unresponsive. Avantika was at a loss trying to guess what had irked him so badly. Eventually, they reached near her apartment.

"Would you mind dropping in for some time?" she asked.

Rashv was surprised at this sudden show of friendship from his dance partner. He was pleased with her gesture but politely refused.

"Thanks but some other day", he waved her goodbye and the auto rickshaw moved forward in the direction of his home.

The next day Avantika eluded Rashv like a plague, even excusing herself from the practice session. Rashv got hold of her after concluding his practice, a couple of hours later, when he saw her at the canteen.

"What's the matter Avantika?" asked Rashv taking a chair opposite her.

"Exactly! What's the matter with you, Rashv? I tried to talk to you yesterday after the practice session and messaged you at night; you even left my phone calls go unanswered and now you are asking me what the matter is." She was literally fuming.

Rashv had not seen Avantika loose her cool even in the most trying of situations while she taught him the dance steps. But this was something else, something like never before. It seemed like she had developed an emotional bond with Rashv, having spent so much time with him and hence could not control her emotions.

Rashv made a sorry face and admitted, "Yeah... I should have called you back. I had gone off to sleep way too early last night and hence could not revert. I checked it in the morning and thought of speaking with you in person today."

Avantika crossed her arms and raised her brow, her expression that of go-on-am-listening; and signalled him to continue.

"Well, actually it's my studies that are troubling me. I have been neglecting them for quite some time. Just as you need dance to be happy, I can't stay away from my books and notes for too long" Rashv tried to make an excuse.

"My dear friend, if that was the case then you should have told me, I would not have pushed you for the extra practice sessions" Avantika replied with concern on her face.

"But had I been partial towards the practice sessions, I would have disappointed you and affected your chances of winning the competition. I know it means more to you than it does to me. But I would not have liked it if you'd have cut a slack in front of the college just because of me. Sorry, that's not how I am."

Avantika could only smile at his words and flushed.

"You are actually a sweet little mushball", she beamed and again reached for his round cheeks. "Okay then let's make a deal. We would not ignore either our studies or our dance practice. You help me with the exams and I will help you out with the dance. What say?" she asked.

"Awesome!" Rashv agreed.

It was the start of a new kind of partnership between the two.

CHAPTER 19

Weeks flew by with Rashv practicing his dance moves and Avantika trying hard to master her accounting skills with his dedicated help. Rashv was enjoying his brand new friendship with Avantika especially the practice sessions after the lectures. During the weekend, they took to their books with a vengeance.

The day for the event was nearing with Avantika managing to make Rashv shake a leg and practice hard so that they may be termed as the best dancing couple. In one of the dance moves, Rashv had to pop Avantika on his thighs and then swivel her around his shoulders and make her land in front of him in a swift move typically known as the 'pop around the back-swing and lift' move. Initially, it gave Rashv the scare of his lifetime when he saw what he was expected to do. He feared he would not be able to lift Avantika properly and worried that he may instead twist her arms and strain her muscles.

"Are you sure you want me to do this?" asked a nervous Rashv.

Avantika nodded with a firm smile on her face. "Remember the first lesson of dance is to trust your partner. And I trust you, Rashv!"

Rashv, on the other hand, was a bit reluctant not just because it was going to be difficult for him but because also because he had sensed Avantika's eagerness in her eyes which was way too much for his comfort. She didn't miss a single opportunity to be around him. Sometimes he felt like she had even begun to like him. Rashv's entire focus, on the other hand, was merely on his mission with his eyes set at destination number 23, with no chance of love blossoming in any way.

THE 23ʳᴰ GIRL

Days went by with Rashv trying to perfect the most difficult move with as much diligence as he could muster. Sometimes he failed to hold her properly and was thus unable to go ahead with the move and at times he was unable to make her land properly on her feet as a result of which, he was unable to balance both himself and Avantika. Even if he succeeded in completing the move, it didn't look elegant. It was performed so slowly and carefully every time that the move struck out like a sore thumb during the entire duration of the dance act.

"Guys, buckle up. Else your entire act will fizzle out and will be over-shadowed by others", expressed the choreographer who had high hopes from both of them.

The D-day was almost nearing and Rashv was invested in the practice with all of his heart and soul. From the proper positioning of his limbs to pull and push movements, the tapping of the foot and the rhythmic cha-chas with the beat, Rashv had mastered it all and they both looked great dancing together to the extent that it seemed that the chemistry between them could have put the stage on fire. On the other hand, Avantika had taken a liking for Rashv over the past few days and she was looking for an appropriate moment to share her feelings with him. On the day of the final rehearsals, just as the session ended, Rashv gave her a twirl around him and as they stood in the final pose with a cheery smile, his hands on her waist and his wild heartbeat sending electric impulses down her body. She went breathless with desire and dragged him to the green room, immediately after the cheer from the audience had died down and the next pair had replaced them on the stage. Inside, she pulled him close and gave him a sensuous kiss on his jawline. Rashv did not have the time to respond as his batch of friends had barged in and invaded their privacy. Avantika managed to slip a small handwritten note in his palm. She had scribbled the note before their performance started, expressing her heartfelt emotions and her desire to take the relationship to the next level.

Even as Avantika's expression of love blazed him to a new heat, Rashv reminded himself that he was on a mission and that he had crossed his heart that he would not take any undue advantage from any of the girls that he met, especially when he did not feel for them as much as they did. The letter from Avantika came as a final signal to press the red button and take a leap towards his destination.

The time had arrived. The annual dance festival had commenced with a bang. The "mismatched-pair" dancing competition was being touted to arouse great interest from the student fraternity as it had many first timers in dancing shoes just like Rashv. It was finally time for their performance with their names being announced on stage. They were welcomed with claps and whistles. Avantika looked extremely attractive and gorgeous in her make-up and costume. They walked hand in hand with Rashv taking a slow and measured step in contrast to Avantika who walked with grace and confidence.

"I'm there. Don't worry", she smiled pressing his hand tightly.

And they began effortlessly, matching their steps to the beats in a synchronized rhythm that could have put a trained dancer to shame. Rashv's swift moon walk alternated with his slow robotic movements and Avantika's constantly changing expression on her face had the crowd in the auditorium cheering loudly for them all along. They had literally set the stage on fire with their elegant and eye-catching moves. And then it was time for the move of the day – the pop around the back-swing and lift move, as they called it. And just when Rashv was about to pop Avantika on his thighs, he deliberately pulled her a bit closer thus landing her onto his stomach and... THUDDD...! The effect was such that both instantly fell onto the ground, with Avantika completely over

Rashv and her nose bleeding profusely. The crowd was left stunned as they had never expected them to falter after showcasing some of the best dance moves of the evening.

"I'm sorry", Rashv pleaded over the phone next day.

"You remember I had said in the beginning itself that trust is the most important factor in dance as well as in life. You failed me in the competition and there is no guarantee that you would not in future. And moreover, the embarrassment that you have caused me is beyond repair. It's all over", blurted a highly agitated Avantika and disconnected the call.

Rashv gave a brooding smile as he placed the letter on the shelf.

CHAPTER 20

Rashv's upper and lower back had been heavily bandaged due to a severe ligament tear from the previous day. He felt a sharp pain in his entire back. It would hurt for several minutes before subduing and then returned in equal measure. But probably the emotional pain of breaking up with Avantika affected him more than the pain from the physical injuries he had sustained. There were several occasions when both of them crossed each other's path inside the college premises but instead of showing concern to each other and asking about the bruises and injuries from the fall, they avoided each other like total strangers. Time does these strange things. It turns strangers into friends and friends into strangers.

'Indeed the biggest tragedy of life is not that we die, but about what dies inside of us while we are still alive.'

The college grapevine spread many stories about them long after that fateful day. However, both of them avoided clarifying anything and were never to be seen together again. They had entrusted their wounds to that age old apothecary called Time which was known to heal all wounds, slowly but surely. Also, due to the fact that the entire crescendo about the college festival had now faded and exams took the center stage for the students, one hardly found any time for tending to personal hurts. Last minute xeroxes, exchanging notes and discussing solutions to important questions took prime importance as a majority of the students burned the midnight lamp and toiled hard for the tests. The final year students were even more pressurized as their exams were due within a month.

Both Rashv and Rahul helped each other in preparing for the final year exams with great gusto and were highly confident about cracking it with a super-duper percentage. The injuries and pain from the fall and the sweet memories of constantly changing expressions of Avantika's face faded sooner than expected as textbooks kept Rashv's heart and mind occupied. The smiles on their faces had been sucked by the annual terror that spreads by sharing of class notes.

The final year examinations came and went in a jiffy just like Rashv's last three years had gone by at college. Over the years there had been a sea change in his personality. He had matured with time and not just in mind, but also in his looks, physique and confidence level. Rashv's sharp numerical abilities had landed him a high paying job in the county's top share marketing portal, right after college. Working in an intense corporate culture for almost three years made him realise the importance of being presentable and more so during client meetings where an overweight person was more often than not considered as being lazy. Hence he decided to transform himself by dedicatedly visiting the gym without fail to stay fit if nothing else. As a result, the soft, fluffy body of his early youth, which was often tagged as that of a "baby elephant" by his friends, was transformed into a lean, muscular frame. Rashv did a world of justice to his sharp features when he lost his excess flab and transformed from a nonchalant teen into a poised youth. His black-rimmed spectacles sitting over his highly chiseled features, neatly done hair and goatee added up to a sleek corporate look which was quite the honey bait for most women around him. That and his sharp business acumen brought him great success at work. Admiration came rolling in from all quarters. Time rolled on quickly for Rashv. He didn't even realise that he had completed three years in the corporate cabin until the congratulatory emails started pouring into his inbox after the annual appraisal exercise. With two promotions, a good pay and overall satisfactory three years in the company, life was going great guns for him.

THE 23RD GIRL

As time flew by, Rashv got his perks of being in several "sort of" relationships one after the other. "Sort of" because his old hurt and his personal obsession with the number 23 made him indulge into several casual relationships which he got in and came out of just as easily. Having shed his boyish weight, he felt ever more comfortable in his skin and was not scared of putting his heart on the line anymore. His dashing looks and open attitude were a magnet for the girls. Sometimes it was tough to end the relationships and he had to shake them off for the flimsiest of reasons. But sometimes he was also saddened by the tragic end that he had to put to a sweet relationship just for the sake of adding up to his number game. Nevertheless, he kept on taking a leap towards his destination and enjoyed each and every moment of his fast lifestyle.

He had been hundreds of kisses deep in relationships with twenty girls over the span of four short years. But his calm demeanor, tailored conversations, and calculative brain helped him keep his sanity even after all the self-inflicted chaos that the meet, date and break-up scenario landed him in. Sometimes he wondered that even Casanova had a slower rate of getting the girls.

Several angry and teary-eyed break-ups later, the shelf in his room was adorned with a string of broken hearts. It was almost full of souvenirs from the girls he had wooed and broken up with. From hand-written letters to confession notes, greeting cards to photographs, chocolate boxes to gifts like artificial rings, ties, cufflinks etc., Rashv had seen a rollercoaster of a time. There was also a box of condoms lying in the far corner of the shelf, unused and nearing the expiration date, probably hyperventilating for Rashv's perfect girl who existed in an uncertain future. Rashv somehow and always managed to wade through the emotional roller coaster life that he had chosen, sometimes coldly trampling on feelings to race ahead towards his destination.

THE 23ᴿᴰ GIRL

Once Rashv simply wondered where all the girls that he had wooed and dated would be. What did he mean to them, after all? Had he not met them would their life be any different as compared to life after having met him? While most of his relationships were casual, some of them held the potential of blossoming into real, stable relationships. But in his mad personal quest, he moved on so fast that those relationships took a dizzy trail past him and added up to nothing but a hazy image from a casual hangover. It had been so many relationships with so many girls that he no more attached any emotional value to any new relationship whatsoever. It was as if not allowing himself the ease and commitment of a stable relationship had turned him into an emotional zombie.

"May I come in Sir?" a petite voice disturbed his time-lapse. It was his personal secretary.

"Yes, Devina... please do and close the door behind you!"

"You see, one has to follow the rulebook in the office", she smiled.

"Rule books can burn in hell. For now tell me the status of our personal trip to Leh?"

"That's what I have come here for. We so deserve a break from the four walls of this office! Don't we?"

After endless discussion and meticulous planning, they finalized the dates and the schedule.

"So, the plan is this: you make a move and I'd follow right after you. After all, what is a boss without his secretary?" She winked.

"You are getting smarter in my company", he chortled.

"By the way, this is for you" she slipped a platinum band towards him across the table.

"Ahh... That's sweet! Thank you, mademoiselle", he winked and smiled with a knowledge of what was coming next as he slipped the ring on his finger.

CHAPTER 21

Rashv swayed his head to the music, eyes closed and sitting all relaxed in the airplane seat.

"Excuse me", a honey-dipped voice cut his solitary trip short and brought him back to the real world with a tug at his shoulder. He looked up as he let out a huge yawn and immediately realized. "Ohh... I'm so sorry. How disrespectful of me to greet a lady with a yawn!"

'I guess I will have to deal with a pretentious fool for the rest of this journey', she arched a supercilious eyebrow at him as she asked him for a pass through to her seat. He stood up, pulled out the earphones and made way for her to take her seat. She shook her head with disgust and took the window seat.

"The world doesn't fail to amuse you every now and then. It has got morons strategically placed all around for the purpose", she muttered under her breath, making herself comfortable.

"Hi! I'm Rashv!"

"Roohi, and I do not like to talk to random strangers."

"The world would be a happier place if you possess kindness and warmth as your default setting", Rashv replied in a sing-song voice, looking towards her with a wide smile plastered on his face.

"I couldn't care less!" She shot back at him with an intimidating look. Rashv cowered back into his seat and simply raised his fingers indicating for peace but the mischievous smile on his face made a comeback and he ran his fingers through his thick mane, switched off his phone and locked his seat belt as per the instructions as he waited for the flight to take off before indulging in a small nap.

THE 23ᴿᴰ GIRL

The constant activity along the aisle unsettled him and woke him up. Lunch was being served to the passengers.

"Veg – with a glass of orange juice", Rashv answered before the air hostess could even ask him about his preference. He was damn hungry and although he hated the food served in flights, he had been looking forward to a meal and wouldn't mind having something to eat at this time.

"Excuse me, pretty lady! And what would you like to have?" Rashv tugged at Roohi's shoulder to wake her up. For a moment he had his eyes fixated on her. For the first time, he saw her at peace without a crease on her forehead. A lock of hair that fell on one side of her left shoulder in soft waves with streaks of honey colored highlights appeared to be a perfect contrast to her glowing porcelain skin. Kohl-lined eyes, a pert nose atop her high cheekbones and glossy pink lips made her look simply ethereal.

"She looks even prettier asleep", he smiled as he felt a temptation to flick back the stray lock of hair that had fallen on her face.

"What the.. hell?" a harsh loud voice fell on his ears and brought him back to an uncomfortable reality.

"Fff... Food? Would you like to order food?" He fumbled with words, having being caught ogling at her shamelessly. 'Was I so mesmerized that I didn't even realise that she had woken up?' He reflected, flushed with shame.

She eyed him suspiciously and once again gave him one of her supercilious looks. She had learned the art of intimidating people to divert unwanted attention. Staying alone, far away from home and family makes most people defensive and she had mastered the art to the core.

"What's wrong with me? Why am I behaving like a hippie? Let me better talk it out with her rather than having her assume things about me." He contemplated while having his dinner but just then the soul-stirring voice fell upon his ears, once again.

"Are you from Mars or from an entirely different universe?" She asked him upon finishing her meal, avoiding an eye contact.

Rashv turned his face slightly towards her with a confused look.

"Hullo, I am asking you!", she added. "I mean what on earth prompted you to dress like as if you are vacationing on a beach and not actually flying on a plane?" She turned her face around only to find Rashv staring at her. She was about to flare up again when she suddenly decided against it and gave up. She did not want to spoil her mood by constantly picking out on the guy sitting next to her. After all, how people dress and behave is their prerogative and one cannot really get them to react in a way that suits one best. She let out a sigh and decided to bear the caricature sitting next to her for the rest of the flight. Quite a test of her patience, she realised, as she was not used to suffering fools with a smile.

On the other hand, Rashv felt himself being helplessly drawn to her allure. It was probably her simple beauty that attracted him the most. Despite wearing a monochrome salwar kameez with a simple hand-woven dupatta balancing around her neck, she looked very attractive. Rashv was so besotted by the beauty sitting beside him that it seemed that nothing at all could bring him back from the land of La La Love. Over the past years he had met and dated several girls who probably did anything to have his attention but none of them had been like her, so self-assured and independent. She was a striking balance between contemporary and traditional. He analyzed and smiled.

She snapped her fingers at him bringing him back from his trance once again.

"The magic of good genes can be visualised upon seeing a

beautiful face, and yours seem to be indeed very good!" he blurted out unthinkingly.

Roohi was startled at the odd reply at first and gave him a stern look. He let out a sheepish little smile even as he realised that maybe he was crossing the line with her.

She decided to play a little further. "You really don't seem to have any decency. Stop behaving like a road side Romeo or else I'll have to call the flight steward and initiate some action against you!" Roohi flared up in a piercing tone. To Rashv, it felt like her sharp tone could probably cut through his eardrum and turn him deaf. He desperately needed to cool off his mind and as such he immediately excused himself to the lavatory. For indeed it wasn't really sensible enough to approach a girl he had met just two hours back, he realised. He splashed some water on his face, allowed his heart and mind to collide with each other in a scruffy battle of words and emerged after a good ten minutes.

Roohi, on the other hand, had been secretly bemused with the way Rashv was flirting with her. Without his knowledge, she even took sideway glances at him at regular intervals. Even though he wasn't dressed appropriately, his well-groomed face, boyish features and well defined muscular body were quite a sight for her. On top of this, his now damp locks made him look sizzling hot. She nevertheless had her mind at place unlike Rashv and chose to be cautious from the outside but her heart had already started melting from the inside. As a result of which she found herself caught at the crossroads.

"God! Why did you create this dumb guy? And even if you had to, why did he have to look like a Greek God! Why?!"

She slid her purple rimmed glasses on her nose as she picked out a notebook from her purse and began to scribble notes. She had been working on a new article, '10 unexplored places in north India' for a leading fashion magazine. It was a pretty recent thing for her, Journalism and free-lancing. She had taken a six-month sabbatical from work to repair her corporate life burnout and focus on her passions as the run-of-the-mill office life had begun to take a toll on her spirits. As she was looking for greater meaning and depth in life, taking control of her own life was one way to save her soul and render some semblance of sanity back into the crazy disorder that her life had become. So over a period of several months into this sabbatical, this enthusiastic electrical engineer with a passion for circuits indulged in two of her dearest activities – lots of traveling with a smattering of writing, her other calling in Life. Being the intelligent, smart and independent kind, she had no respect for shallowness and the people who were overflowing with it. And here was this guy, sitting next to her, so irresistibly attractive but so very much like a clown that she found it hard to keep a straight face in his presence.

Rashv came back and sat by her side. "I am sorry. I think I must have disturbed you. I wouldn't bother you anymore", he gave her a flat smile.

"Ha... as if I needed your confirmation", replied Roohi placing his hat back on his seat, looking all agitated. She plugged her earphones and turned her gaze away looking out of the window.

Rashv, at this point in time, understood that from here on things might take an ugly turn much against his liking and decided to keep quiet till the flight landed.

"I am sorry", he meekly admitted.

Roohi smiled at Rashv's words still looking the other way, at the tinge of light that she could see below, flying from the altitude.

Rashv heaved a sigh of relief upon landing in Delhi. They alighted from the flight separately. It was as if the mixed feelings of attraction and that of being uncomfortable were too much of emotional overload for Roohi. She picked up her stuff and started to leave. Their eyes met for a fleeting moment and then they parted... into separate ways that diverged like a two-way street. But that one look, across an aisle of strangers, was the only moment that would matter for both of them for the days to come as none of them knew anything about the other except for each other's names and the fact that they were irresistibly drawn towards one another. For you would agree, dear reader, how strange it feels to have met a stranger, feel like they meant something to you and then go back to being strangers... once again. After all, there is an overwhelming amount of guilt one needs to deal with when you just decide to let people go, slip away from your fingers like dry sand.

Apart from the spark that they hid from each other throughout the flight, one thing that Rashv was probably ignorant of was that the two hours in the flight had literally turned him into a butt, what with those clothes he had decided to wear for the flight and then again for acting like someone who apparently had no connection between his mind and tongue. As a result of this, he made abrupt confessions of his feelings to Roohi and ended up looking like a total fool. He decided to spend the next seven hours at the airport, a stopover before the connecting flight took him to Leh, his vacation destination. He took a stroll all around the terminal before settling in the waiting lounge with the latest business issue of the Fortune magazine, a cup of hot latte and a McDonald's burger. He did become the center of attention for the rest of the travelers at the terminal too with his Hawaiian look but he seemed to be unfazed by all the unnecessary attention. Instead, his mind continued to drift towards Roohi every now and then. He cursed himself for making an underwhelming impression of himself in front of her. And moreover, he was disheartened that the least he could do was to bid her good-bye, which he hadn't.

THE 23RD GIRL

Rashv decided to give his thoughts, mind and heart a break. He took out his buzzing phone to check who it was. It was his personal secretary at the office. After missing countless calls and text messages, he finally decided to text her back with a very small message.

"I had to change my plans. Please cancel your trip."

His mind was on an entirely different plane now.

Rashv made good use of the early morning connecting flight to Leh by snoring his heart out; much to his co-passengers anguish. The short nap in the flight gave him just enough time to recuperate from the disastrous two hours that he had spent inside the previous flight.

Chapter 22

"Gosh! What a character!" Roohi exclaimed as she took the back seat of the prepaid taxi on her way to her friend's apartment. It was already sunset time and a beautiful calmness had set on the landscape. As the taxi sped from the airport out on the highway, she felt a strange mix of emotions. She felt relieved to have finally reached her destination and a bit restless as she somehow felt like she had made all kinds of wrong choices in the last couple of hours. It felt like she had chosen silence over words, coldness over contact and bashfulness over what she had always been looking for - a true connection which she kind of sensed in Rashv's eyes at the time of their parting. Could he have been more than what she thought him to be?

She was yet to come out of the weird spell that Rashv had cast upon her. There was something in him which made her think of him long after they had parted. Was it about his physical appearance, his deep masculine voice or was it the intensity in his eyes that made her go weak in the knees and made her stomach turn up in knots whenever she recalled catching his eye? Some stranger in the flight that she met and did not even get acquainted with enough to share contact details with was now constantly on her mind. That's the thing about flying; you could talk to someone for hours and then never see them again.

Roohi... Just like her name, she was always the girl with a soul. She had always trodden the path of her dreams in life. When she was younger, she was passionate about studies and chose the company of her textbooks over everything else, to the extent that she was happy being labeled by her frustrated friends as an 'incorrigible bookworm'. Roohi's parents were academics and as such, there was no dearth of good books at home. As a kid, she had a strange pull towards the world of

109

science and there was nothing in the world that she valued more than a quiet corner of the house and her books. A high-flying career as an engineer was her only aim and she didn't mind sacrificing the customary 'happening life' of regular teenagers which people of her age would die to have.

Ever since her school days, Roohi would keep a replica of an airplane at her study desk to remind herself about her eventual goal of becoming a successful engineer. Sometimes she even regretted out rightly rejecting some of the most handsome looking potential dates but soon she would quash any deviations caused by her notorious hormones and shifted her focus back on her books and dreams. As a result of her pinpointed focus and determination, by the time college ended, she had already landed a lucrative job. She began the endless climb of the corporate ladder but her relentless dedication to work and frequent overextension of her boundaries eventually led her to a work burnout resulting in mental and emotional exhaustion within a matter of few years. At this point of time, with the help of her well-meaning parents, friends and the family doctor, she decided to slow down and take a break. Thankfully, the company policy allowed her a six-month sabbatical which she begrudgingly took at the behest of the well-wishers and then later found it as the golden opportunity to explore and sort out her life by indulging in her passions. She took to extensive travelling and began to blog about it, sometimes even writing small articles and freelancing for popular magazines. This time apart from work gave her an opportunity to rediscover her priorities and interests. With the solitude that the sabbatical offered her, she often missed the company of a nice partner and wondered if life would be a tad bit easier or meaningful if shared with a significant other. In other words, she began to crave for a stable relationship.

And then, just as she met Rashv, the balloon of emotions and feelings locked deep inside her since long was let loose which started creating havoc within her tiny heart. Never before had anyone so unabashedly let out his feelings for her and that too without the slightest of hesitation which caught her interest at first. "Either he had the guts to pour his heart out at first instance or maybe he was just plain silly", she analysed. But either way, she was already smitten with his looks and his outspokenness. "Could he have proposed to me had the flight not landed for some more time?" She thought as she imagined of the ways Rashv could have proposed her in a flying aircraft and how she would have reacted.

"Take it easy, Roohi baby", cautioned her mind as the taxi came to a screeching halt in front of an apartment. She rushed out and joined her squealing friends in a group hug. All of them were meeting up after a long gap of almost one year.

"Damn! You look good! What's that tiny little secret that you have managed to hide from your friends? Are you in love!? Why don't I know about it?" her best friend Shikha teased her.

Roohi rolled her eyes and said, "No babes! I was born beautiful!"

Everyone burst into peals of laughter.

"Ya Ya, of course, who can deny that. By the way, where did you get these streaks done? They look so sexy on you!" they continued with their chatter as Roohi picked up her luggage with the help of her friends and moved into the lift.

It was catch-up time for the girls. The four friends; Meghna, Shikha, Roohi and Priya had been the thickest of friends since college. They were the inseparable friends that nothing including time and circumstance could tear apart. Especially Shikha. Shikha and Roohi had been friends since childhood. They went to the same school, then they managed to join the same college and thereafter moving away for work to different parts of the country did not affect their relationship one bit. Meghna and Priya were software professionals in New Delhi while Shikha was working as an assistant manager for a telecom company in Indore. They had been together through the toughest and the happiest of times together.

The friends had gathered in Priya's apartment in New Delhi and had planned to leave by the early morning train for mountain trekking to Himachal Pradesh and further by a road trip to Markha Valley in Jammu. It was exciting to catch up for an adventure with old friends.

At night, after the gossips had died down and everyone was drowsy and retreated for sleep, Roohi was wide awake. Flashes of Rashv's face kept her constant attention as she turned sides and tossed in her bed every now and then. To get her to sleep, she even tried switching on her side of the bedroom lights and reading a romance fiction she had brought along with her. However the more she read, the more she equated the main characters in the novel with herself and Rashv. She was finding it a bit tough to keep her thoughts in check and forget those two hours she had shared with him. It was getting unbearable. She pressed a pillow on her head in a futile attempt to shut out his thoughts but the most she achieved with that was to wake her dear friend up from her shallow sleep.

"What's the matter, Roohi baby? Everything's okay?" Shikha touched her shoulder and asked, all concerned.

"Nothing, it's all very weird. Complicated in fact." Roohi narrated the incidents of the day and shared her feelings and dilemma with her best friend. Her school girl kind of crush on Rashv had turned her into a puddle of hopeless mush. It was indeed senseless to keep thinking of a guy whom she had met on a flight and would never see again. They talked about him till the wee hours of the morning and it was almost time for everyone to wake up.

Shikha hugged her and looked into her eyes. "It's okay, baby.

I am sure you would be able to forget him very soon. What else can you do?"

Roohi nodded in agreement as they slipped into the bed and caught an hour of sleep before the hustle and bustle began and it was time for everybody to pick up the bags and leave.

CHAPTER 23

Rashv reached the hotel room and took the liberty of allowing his weary self a lavish sleep after having a sumptuous dinner. He was so drained after a long overnight put at the airport that his eyes did not open until five o' clock the next morning and he slept for a good ten hours. As he drew the curtains to let the morning rays in, he found the view from the hotel room to be totally breath-taking. The mountains and valleys were covered in snow and small trees dotted the scenery. One strong cup of coffee later, unable to control his wanderlust, he decided to catch a bit of the early morning sun and take a stroll in the nearby Tibetan market.

Rashv spread his arms out, closed his eyes and inhaled the fresh air that welcomed him to one of the most wonderful places on Earth to get lost in and be found. Leh was the most beautiful tick off on his bucket list for the year. His enthusiasm upon visiting Leh and accomplishing a thing on his bucket list was quite apparent as he clicked pictures with the locals there, chatted with them and purchased as many things as he could. He returned to his room quite late in the evening with beautiful memories and a bagful of items that he had collected.

A couple of days later, Rashv reached the next spot on his itinerary - Uleytokpo, an enchanting village about 70 kilometers west to Leh, located at an altitude of about 10,000 ft. It is a small town located in the center of Leh and is considered to be the ideal spot for acclimatizing with Leh. With his travel guide in the right pocket of his snow jacket, Rashv moved out armed with the basic accessories of a traveller... a trekking stick, a camera and sunglasses. He had read all the Do's and Don'ts of trekking from his collection of Travel guide books. At a high altitude there is a high risk of snow blindness and as such, he ensured to keep an additional pair of sunglasses in the event of losing or breaking one. The color of the sky in this piece of heaven he found himself in was stupendous. Though initially, the cool climate gave him slight shivers but soon he got adjusted to the chilly weather and bared himself to the soulful beauty of his surroundings. As he stood under the enormous sky gazing and admiring the serene view, he felt an eternal calmness grow within.

At night, he thought of refreshing the evening's memories as he sat with his camera reviewing his clicks. He was glancing through the shots when one of his clicks generated a fair amount of interest in him as compared to the rest. He brought the camera closer to his eyes and zoomed till the picture flirted with pixelation. He blinked his eyes. Once. Twice. Thrice. And squealed with delight. "Roohi! Here, in Leh! That can't be possible", his rational brain tried to calm down his pulsating heart. "Is my mind playing games once again? Is she actually here? If yes, then in which hotel?"

Rashv's mind was bustling with two conflicting thoughts. An uncomfortable tension greeted him by the night as he kept tossing on the mattress. Earlier, in the pursuit of his destination no. 23, he had spent sleepless nights imagining himself with girls he had set his eyes on but later that turned to be passé as each time it became an emotionless game for him. However, this time around everything seemed different. She was special and he knew it from the start, from the minute his eyes met hers. He felt a helpless pull towards her as if there were invisible strings attached to his heart that was being tugged towards her. His heart which he had over time moulded into a rock which could neither break nor melt in order to achieve his destination was already shaken to the core. In fact, it had already started melting in the fire of her alluring beauty and captivating charm. Even the ancient and artistically crafted monastery in the backdrop seemed washed out to Rashv in front of Roohi's beautiful face. He simply failed to comprehend what magic she had cast on him and that too in such a brief meeting.

"It must be destiny, of course! We have a chance to meet again", he smiled.

"What is more beautiful, the view here or her face that I cannot rid my mind of?" He sighed as he realised that he couldn't answer the questions that kept revolving in his mind.

Around late evening, Rashv perched near the door of his camping tent with a harmonica in his hand and started playing it. The open sky and cool wind made it a perfect evening for him. Rashv kept on playing tunes on his tremolo tuned harmonica. Nothing stopped him that night. His soul was taken captive by Roohi's thoughts and under that influence, he played soft romantic tunes to calm his uneasy heart.

"Rashv?" a soft voice called out to him in the darkness.

"Wow! So now I can even hear you calling me out! I have actually started hallucinating. One of the most prominent signs of falling in love with someone", he chuckled.

Rashv realised that he indeed missed her terribly. His heart raced furiously and he lost his focus on playing the mouth organ. The melody came out half baked and eventually he had to stop playing midway. He got a bit agitated as he didn't like to stop midway while playing his mouth organ.

"Rashv?"

He pressed both his hands on his ears thinking that he was hearing voices again, as if visualizing her wasn't enough for him.

"RASHV?!" This time the voice was hoarse. He opened his eyes in utter disbelief. Initially, he chose to ignore it and brushed it as a figment of his imagination. But with the figure standing in front of him, he eventually realised that it was for real.

THE 23RD GIRL

It was Roohi indeed, standing right in front of him!

"Roohi!" Exclaimed Rashv in delight, as he stood up and threw both his arms around her in a tight embrace.

Roohi was a bit startled by this sudden display of affection and before she could ask him anything Rashv uttered, parting away, looking straight into her eyes, "Never thought that I would meet you again. And like this..! I am one happy backpacker right now under the light of these million stars", he made no attempt to hide his adulation for her.

She stood still, too surprised, with words failing her again. 'Wow! I can't believe I was missing this guy!' she thought to herself and smiled. No one had ever been so unabashed about his adoration for her... and with such audacity! It was getting difficult for her to breathe properly and even stand in a balance. Her heart was hammering hard on her ribs and her insides had melted into a mush. A tsunami of emotions kept hitting her heart and she flushed.

She decided to give her heart a free hand and asked her mind to simply shut up and stop reasoning with her this time.

"Are you always this frank with everyone?" She asked him after regaining her senses.

"I don't really know. I don't get myself much these days", he replied.

Roohi's heart simply melted at his soul-stirring smile. She let out a laughter that resembled a soft tinkling of bells.

"How could one not fall in love with this girl", Rashv thought. Her curls were playing with the wind in the moonlit night. "True beauty", he whispered under his breath.

"What did you just say!" she cross-checked.

"Nothing, it just feels nice to meet someone familiar at this altitude", he tried to put up an excuse.

"Yeah, that's true! Sorry, I forgot to ask you. How come you are here?"

"It has got nothing to do with following you, I swear! I have not been following you", he teased her and continued. "On a more serious note, I just wanted to take a break from the office and cool off. I had planned this trip quite a few months back. What about you?"

"Would you believe if I said I am here for just the same reasons? Well, actually I too am on a break from work and Leh was one of my stopping points for the sake of the travel article I am writing these days on unexplored places in northern India. You know my father is a Dendrochronologist. He has been to Leh quite a few times and recommended me to explore it for the article."

"Wow! That's pretty cool I must say!" Rashv beamed. "But... what was that big word that you just used to describe what your father does?"

"A Dendrochronologist... is a scientist who studies climate changes and past events influencing it by comparing the successive annual growth rings formed concentrically inside trees and old timber. My father has made several research trips to Leh in reference to climate change and the corresponding melting of glaciers in the Himalayas."

Rashv was impressed with the glacier talk, even as he pretended to not be blinded by science and fancy concepts she was talking about and replied, "Damn! Really? And how is that done?"

"You know how we celebrate our birthday every year by adding another candle to our cakes? Well, trees do it by adding one more ring around their core. If you pull out a section of the tree from the center, you can identify its age. The number of rings on its center indicates the age of a tree. And the thickness of the rings indicates the growth of the tree during the year which in turn is affected by climate. So basically my father can tell you the climate change patterns for as far back as 2000 years or more by just looking at old tree samples", she explained, moving her fingers in an animated way.

"Awesome! Like father like daughter", he smiled.

"Haha! Thankyou!" Roohi giggled at the compliment.

"Anyway, I know it's a bit odd but I and my friends are staying in a camp nearby. Why don't you join us tomorrow? Let's explore Leh together!?" she proposed.

"Ohh, I would love that for sure!" Rashv replied. They continued to talk for several hours seated on a large rock in front of his tent till the stars in the sky slowly started disappearing in the faint light of the cracking dawn. This new familiarity budding between the two was a clear contrast to their last meeting in the airplane which was a total opposite of this meeting.

CHAPTER 24

The soothing rays of the early morning sun were peeking from behind the woolly clouds that were being blown by the wind across the horizon. Roohi's friends had set up a landscape telescope to explore the beautiful panorama of rolling clouds and the natural beauty around them. They were sitting in a circle and were all talking when she showed up at the camp along with Rashv. The first reaction of the trio was an expression of disbelief and utter shock.

"What the... hell? Who's that dude with her?" Megha whispered to Shikha. "I bet you know. I caught you two cooking up something till late in the night day before! What's going on here? If you have got anything to do with this, Shikha, I swear... I am going to kill you both for keeping secrets with us", she jeered.

"Dude, I Swear! I seriously had no clue about this!" Shikha defended herself.

Roohi had barely managed to introduce Rashv to their group when the three friends dragged her to the tent and bombarded her with queries. Especially Shikha, who was highly intrigued by this unlikely meeting and was in the eye of a storm for apparently holding back a secret from the other girls. Roohi managed to silence her friends' curiosity by telling them her story in bits and pieces. However, they simply could not believe the one in a million probabilities of two acquaintances meeting up in a location like this, actually happening. Initially, there was a lot of hushed talk about Rashv's presence in Leh and they took a while to adjust to the presence of an unexpected stranger in the group but they soon agreed to include Rashv in their itinerary plans after the customary greetings were exchanged.

"Rashv, have you ever been on a trek before?" Megha tried to break the ice with the newcomer.

It was like someone had asked Rashv to talk about something closest to his heart and he began to give the group a detailed account of his trekking experiences.

"Oh yes, I have been to the Himalayas before on three group treks to Sankri and one solo trek to Kedarkantha. My last trek was to the Kedarkantha and it was one of the most challenging treks that I have ever made and more so because I went for it by myself. He began to tell his story in great detail which made all the girls sit up and take notice.

"Wow! That sounds tough", Roohi was spellbound. She had not expected Rashv to have such an adventurous streak.

"It was tough. By the time I reached the base camp, I felt completely drained as had I missed my breakfast that morning. I was so low on energy, it was hard for me to take even a single step forward. I fuelled myself at the base camp and began to climb to the summit. Having resolved to reach my aim, I did not give up and finally reached the summit by the end of the day. It is one of the most fantabulous feelings in the world, I tell you! That moment when you are on top of the world, you are simply awe-struck and you keep on thinking that it can't be for real. But then you realise, it is real! And it is one of the most beautiful things one can see! It's majestic... the way the mountain ranges yield into one another and glisten with the yellow light from the sun. Snow animals and forest vegetation make for quite a sight. One particular sight from my first trekking experience that I simply cannot forget is that of a big, orange moon shining above the opposite summit. I can't tell you how perfect it was. It was beautiful. It was all worth it", he smiled.

His audience was awestruck by his experiences. They were extremely impressed. Roohi on the other hand, sat watching the discussion come to life as Rashv narrated several other stories from his travel escapades and had the group in a bind.

She noticed him very closely and loved how his eyes shone with a happy spark and how beautiful he thought his journeys had been. She felt a whole lot of love for this man here for the passion that she saw in his eyes and she gauged that he was a man who would follow a difficult thing to the end, come what may and felt immensely attracted to him for it.

"Oh, by the way, that also reminds me, we should have something to eat now. We don't want to go the half distance and turn back due to loss of stamina", Rashv reminded the group.

Roohi put peanut butter on slices of bread and cut them into diagonal pieces. She was totally smitten with Rashv and tried to hold back a shy smile as she felt all fuzzy inside in his presence. It was good to know that he amounted to something beyond his good looks. She had never appreciated men without substance, anyway. And all this talk about strength and stamina was turning her on, sending a rose blush to her cheeks every now and then.

After a hearty breakfast, they decided to start their expedition to the remote, untouched valleys of Uleytokpo. They decided that their first touch point would be the local monastery, located on the top of a small mountain, situated about 12 kilometers from their camp. They decided to rent bicycles and ride along the Indus River and then ride all the way back to their camp in Uleytokpo.

The terrain was largely flat, although there were slight undulations along the way that kept their journey exciting. They followed a narrow trail, cycling one behind the other, giving one another the ego kick about not taking the beaten path. Sometimes the path would get dangerous, with a rock wall at one end and gorges on the other at which point they used to get off from the bicycles and move carefully, in a line. The view down below was breathtaking. For each round they took around the mountain, looking down below gave them a strange rush. Rashv registered every single detail about the journey... from dense forest vegetation to the mesmerizing waterfalls, the restless water of the cool streams rushing down from the mountains, colorful birds to the smell of the dew on the grass they crushed under their feet. Hunchbacked couples held hands to negotiate the steep climb to the monastery. People waved at cute looking mountain kids with straw buckets strung on their heads as they continued their quest. It was mid-July and the weather was perfect owing to little showers on the previous day. They parked their bikes at the base of a small mountain and began to walk towards the monastery which was visible at a small distance now.

The sun had begun to go over to the other side of the horizon. Nevertheless, it was still very cool and bright at the hills, a very beautiful day indeed. Clouds flitted by the peaks of nearby mountains and it looked like as if they had been walking in a dream. Rashv and Roohi had taken a natural inclination towards each other. They gravitated towards one other every once in a while. Tired, their friends separated themselves from them and let the two walk with each other.

They reached the monastery at around noon. It was quite old and held a very peaceful aura. It had a Tibetan architecture and was decorated with strings of colored paper and the atmosphere showcased a vibrant display of colors and old mountain culture. Within the monastery, a larger than life copper-gilt statue of Lord Buddha attracted their attention and they moved to the courtyard where several monks sat, contemplating enlightenment. Various small stupas covered in gold and silver foil, built around the statue were being worshipped with incense. A group of monks was also seen chanting mantras, sitting in front of the statue of the revered teacher, Padmasambhava. The entire experience bought a lot of peace to their weary minds and transcended them to an otherworldly experience. They decided to sit under the tall ancient oak tree growing outside the main stupa and soak in the spiritual experience. It strangely felt like meditation even though none of them had ever had a mindful experience ever before in their lives. They sat in the   padmasana with their hands joined in reverent prayer before the statue of the Buddha.

Suddenly their composure was disturbed by a group of strange men dressed in mustard yellow and burgundy dresses with huge masks on their faces. They were performing to the sound of indigenous musical instruments. Some masked monks were even wearing horns, multicolored ribbons and brocade which shone brightly in the July sun. They came around them and realised that it was the second day of the annual Leh Hemis festival and the dancers were actually Lamas who had gathered together for the annual festival held in reverence of the great teacher Padmasambhava. They squealed in delight. They were in the midst of one of the oldest traditional carnivals of Leh celebrated in the 300-year-old monastery! Serendipity! It was a bizarre but a beautiful feeling to land in the midst of a great spiritual fest, just by plain coincidence. Life lands you such pearls at times.

Roohi looked at Rashv and witnessed a childlike excitement gleaming in his eyes. This star-crossed meeting at Leh had given her several insights into his nature and she felt like he was a far cry than had met her eye in that unforgettable plane flight where they both squirmed in each other's company and barely spoke to each other. She felt a surge of adoration for him but resisted her emotions and joined her friends in watching the lamas celebrate.

It was already evening and there was no way they could have made their way to their camp and so they decided to stay at the monastery overnight and begin the return journey early next morning. The sun had begun to cast a crimson shade over layers of purple on the horizon. The friends had gathered in a small natural park located outside the monastery. It was a beautiful spot to watch the sun resign its yellow shade to the pale moon peeking from behind the trees on the mountain top.

Rashv ran his fingers over the tall grass nonchalantly as they both looked at the sunset. His heart fluttered as Roohi's silky tresses brushed against his arm with every blow of the evening breeze. She was standing on a small rock, her porcelain skin was washed in the soft yellow light of the sun. He closed his eyes and let the moment sink in.

"Hey! You are so quiet. Do you get quiet when you are hiding something?" he finally broke the silence that had settled in comfortably between them.

"Are words necessary at this point? Isn't the sunset here just so beautiful, Rashv?" she smiled back at him and turned her gaze back to the sunset.

"Yeah, it looks like a dream! I love sunsets!" he filled his lungs with the fresh mountain air and continued. "Looking at this beautiful sunset from over a hilltop, attending one of the biggest cultural extravaganzas by sheer stroke of luck, exploring the beauty of these majestic mountains and then standing here, with you, at this point where nothing else matters to me except for the fact that this moment is for real and you are right by my side.. all of this feels like a dream from which I never want to wake up!" Rashv was now looking straight into her eyes. "Roohi, I have loved you from the moment I have met you. I know that everything that I am saying right now comes as a surprise to you and you may be thinking what took me so long to admit my feelings for you", he locked his fingers with his and then looked up again and continued, "We met as strangers for just two hours in a flight and I never hoped to see you again. I buried my feelings so deep into my heart that I learned to live with them, without knowing that they existed or caring to find that they did. I would have lost myself just like any other casualty that happens with us over a period of a lifetime. Hearts break, people lose their sanity and over a period of time, they slowly forget what caused them pain. But you came and spared me the pain of carrying an unspoken love in my heart for the rest of my life. You saved me Roohi. You saved my life. Perhaps all this life that I have lived so far was nothing more than a dream about living because everything makes so much more sense now, that you are with me."

Roohi was left spellbound by Rashv's sudden declaration of love. She lowered her eyes with a shy smile, in a silent acceptance of sharing the same feeling with him. He leaned in closer, his muscles flexing as he bent an elbow to hold her by her waist and traced his hand across her back to simultaneously tangle his fingers in her velvety hair while holding her with the other. Roohi felt such a heady ecstatic rush in her body that it felt that her heart could explode at this moment. Rashv bent forward and kissed her cheek in a soft kiss that melted her body from inside. She was left immobilized in that silent moment of Love. It felt as if she had been transported to another world as Rashv tenderly kissed her eyes, her forehead and her face and then as if following a natural progression, his lips found hers and he planted a deep kiss on her parted lips. She let out a soft moan. For several electrifying moments, she could not understand who was breathing for whom as the kiss deepened and she felt her toes curl and insides burn with a passionate desire. Her knees turned weak and she found it extremely difficult to continue to stand. She pulled away from the kiss and hugged Rashv in a deep embrace as they fell on the grass, and made passionate love to each other, hearts hammering hard on each other's ribcages as they consummated their love and fell asleep in the dew. Everything was perfect. The pale blue moon shone happily above the horizon and the soft breeze caressed their bodies as they lay locked in a tight hug in the tall grass.

"Just because you had me on your back yesterday screaming

that I was forever yours, do not take me for granted, ever", Roohi warned Rashv in a mock anger and they both laughed.

"Of course, my love" Rashv beamed a heart-warming smile at her as he planted a peck on her cheek and helped prepare breakfast for all of them. Next on the list was white water rafting and Art Cafe hopping to collect souvenirs and memories from the trip, not to say that they needed any souvenirs to remember their time together as now they were a couple and their time together had been unforgettable, to say the least. Time flew by following the inscrutable Law of Relativity as it always does when one is having a good time and finally it was time to say goodbye. They parted, but with the promise of a lifetime companionship.

CHAPTER 25

"Well…" Rahul said, looking up at Rashv. "How was it?"

"Lip smackingly wet!" Rashv replied with a wink.

"Yikes!" Rahul made a range of noises indicating disgust. "Cheap guy!" he nagged Rashv to spill beans over other details of their meeting but Rashv was simply not forthcoming with the info which led Rahul to eventually leave the topic in frustration.

"Did she cry when you guys parted?" he asked Rashv.

"She did not just cry. She was heartbroken that we had to part. For the entire ride from our camp to Leh station, she wept her eyes out. Look at my T-shirt. It is still stained with the kohl from her eyes" Rashv sighed remembering their moment of separation.

"Or maybe the reason why she cried so much is that you are just a disappointingly plain, bad kisser!" Rahul mimicked a tone of sympathy and at this point, Rashv had to shoo him away. He had just returned home and was dead tired to put himself up to any kind of mischief. He took a quick shower and laid in the bed but surprisingly he could not get one careless moment of sleep. His sleep had been replaced by flashes of the time he had spent with Roohi. Her beautiful face and tinkling laughter kept him sleepless yet again, causing a whirlwind in his heart and mind. He decided to put through a call to her… once, twice, thrice. The number was unavailable.

"Nevermind. She must not have reached yet." He reasoned and decided to get some much-needed sleep. As he turned off the lights and turned over to sleep, he had a flash of realisation… Rashv froze in shock. Everything was perfect. He had just found a perfect partner. They were so happy.

And then, on the other hand, there was this old game he had been playing in his life. It felt all meaningless in front of the happiness he had found. For the first time ever, he felt silly. He denied reality. He held his face in his hands and kept repeating, "It can't be. It just can't be!"

"Is this love for Roohi so strong that I have forgotten my game of fate altogether? Am I going to take a pit-stop at destination number 22? Can she still be the right one for me?"

Rashv had suddenly found himself at an unexpected crossroads in life. His conscience pricked him constantly. "Am I going to completely shelve my resolve to meet the 23rd girl, find my soulmate and win the game of fate or am I going to surrender to the love of my life, Roohi?"

For the second time around in his life, he was being tormented by a number which he thought had dominated his whole life. Life had indeed worked out around his superstition. But this one instance of having met Roohi turned over all his theories. He began to reason with himself. "Was this merely an odd superstition? Am I right in still following it? Is it something that I can just brush aside? Regardless of how it has always been? Regardless of how right everything feels right now? Could life really be straight jacketed to fit around the number at all times?" He wondered as to whether he had surrendered his life decisions blindly to a number and if he should stop somewhere. Someday? Today? Now? At this point, with Roohi in his life? Roohi had come and changed everything. She was forcing him to challenge the meaning the number held in his life even though his initial reaction after his discovery was that of fear and guilt. Rashv was fearful of choosing her even when she felt like destiny, because in his mind, destiny was only a number. Silly as it felt, Rashv simply could not decide what to do at this point in life. Abandon a game of numbers he began in his reckless youth or continue with the tide and take charge of his life, come what may.

He had no answers to the dilemma. Life felt like a breeze with Roohi. It was such a harmonious relationship that it felt as if he had found his soulmate. During the entire relationship, not even once did the thought of his game of fate come across his mind as he was totally smitten by love, totally absorbed in her. He was amazed that his heart that had grown rock solid over the years had melted like an ice-cream in her love without leaving any space for reason and logic. Love indeed is the mysterious force that puts a full stop to all logical and critical thinking powers one has, he realised.

His now awakened mind reasoned that if he chose Roohi, it would be criminal to those girls with whom he had broken up just for the sake of his number theory and put a full stop to the relationships, only for the game to progress and eventually reach its endpoint. The logic of following the number had passed his test several times in life. As he looked back on his life, he realised that following the number had indeed brought him good luck. To the extent that he attributed his success completely to the number. He remembered where he had started his journey and made several mental references to his past. Life had drastically changed after university days. He was elated when he saw the number 23 engraved on the gold medal which he had received from the university and more importantly it was on the 23rd of September when he joined the corporate world and the result was in front of him. His life had completely turned around in a matter of years. His heart ached as he finally decided that he would have to put a full stop to his relationship with Roohi, however much he loved her as she was only the 22nd girl and not the 23rd one as he had promised himself to settle in life with. It seemed so stupid to him thinking of how naive he was in those days when a slight bruise to his ego made him undertake this unusual path and how he was even more stupid to follow it to this day. Was he so blinded by his own superstition? Even if he was, he realised that the only thing that had always kept him going on in his pursuit was his belief in the way his life was inextricably woven around the number 23. He had to follow it, he told himself.

Soon, Rashv began to evade Roohi as much as he could by giving various excuses. He didn't seem to be the Rashv that Roohi had known from day one. She felt that something more important weighed in on Rashv and she didn't know what it was. She was sure that it was not his work that made him drift away from her, for he was considered as the best employee in his company. Also, she did not think that it was a casual relationship they had or a one-night affair which he could easily get over after reaching his hometown. Nor did she expect it to be a case of a see-saw relationship between them in which the lovers eventually part ways. She did not suspect that there could have been some ex-lover suddenly appearing and creating a rift between them. However much she tried to reason out his erratic behavior, she simply couldn't comprehend the reason. There was a time when she had vouched for lovers like them and prayed for their tribe to increase so that the world would always be filled with love. But her faith in her simplistic view had started to dwindle when her calls and messages were left unanswered for long.

Rashv started dropping subtle hints to Roohi through short messages. That he was forced to put his relationship to a slow death by his very own hand turned him into a sad man. He turned silent and lost his joie de vivre till his forever gloomy face and bloodshot eyes became reason enough for his mother to intervene. The extremity of his sadness made her feel like she would never be able to see the old Rashv again, at least not until a long time.

Roohi, on the other hand, felt like a lifeless soul dancing to the tunes of life. Life is a bitch and Love is the mother-in-law of all bitches, she realised. Never had she thought that Rashv would let her down. She never thought that he would ever hurt her and leave her all of a sudden when things were going smooth. Darkness had fallen all around her. Her heart turned frigid, she was alive for the world but dead from within. Any form of emotions ceased to exist in her.

Sometimes in between the crazy madness of everyday life, love leads us to a perfect fairy tale but an unexpected break-up simply sucks out life from you. Days and nights seemed meaningless to her and so did her work as she abstained herself from everything she liked to do. It had all been so short-lived that she had not even been able to finish the article on Leh when her dreams began to shatter. She had enough material to write about, but no spirit. She could not believe that something she held so valuable could turn so hollow so soon. She became dull and lifeless and she simply sat at home with her cell phone in hand in anticipation that Rashv would call one day, everything would be fine and they would be together again. She felt as if it was just yesterday that they had been so close but it wasn't the reality anymore. The reality was that it had been almost a month that Rashv had stopped replying completely to her messages and calls. She felt suffocated thinking about her lovely relationship which had died an unexpected, unceremonious death. Roohi still couldn't come to terms with her broken relationship and Rashv's unexplained goodbyes. She started hallucinating about Rashv until her parents decided to fly her to Dubai to her uncle's place with the hope that a change of scene would cure her bleeding heart.

CHAPTER 26

"Priya, please set the presentation for the board meeting."

There was no way Rashv could have got Roohi off his mind without immersing himself in his work again.

The thing about heartbreak is that... you may not realise it, but it's permanent. You may choose to immerse yourself in books, music, work, art, alcohol or invest your heart again in a different partner with a rebound relationship but you kind of never recover from a good relationship that fell apart. You may think that putting up brick after brick of stone wall around your heart and isolating yourself may help, but the truth is, in the end, it's only as strong as a sand castle. One crushing memory of them and everything comes toppling down. You may even try changing your heart's setting from warm to freezing cold but that too does not take the occasional sting away from the memory of the long-dead relationship. Love hurts and breaking your own heart into a million pieces hurts even more. There are hundreds of things one stops doing and thousands of places one stops going to, just because they remind you of your old, lost love. And so was the case with Rashv. His effervescent personality had changed overnight. Despite his mental calculations of how Roohi was actually not the right one for him as she was only the 22nd girl in his life and not the 23rd as he had wanted, his heart told him that it never felt more right and more complete about any other person he had ever met but his calculative mind always won the constant tug of war with his heart. Somehow he managed to live through his days hoping for the wound to turn old and diminish in feeling. But the road ahead was long and laborious.

It was the annual general meeting of the board of directors and Rashv was in charge of the presentations.

"All the best! We begin in ten", said Priya, his partner and co-worker as she flashed a quick smile at him.

As they went on with the presentation and the number crunching, Rashv cast a spell on his seniors by the incisiveness and depth of his knowledge and the range of his proposals to steer the company forward and take the competitors head on.

"Success is a journey, not a destination. Gentlemen, there are many companies in the country which provide Portfolio Management Services, Wealth Management, Insurance, Demat Account Services, Money Transfer and others. Our edge is that we are not exclusive to one service but we provide these facilities along with stock broking, IPO services, Share registry, mutual fund registry and many more financial products all under a single roof. So today, even though we stand tall as the industry leader in financial products distribution, among the top five in the country for stock broking services and among the top three offering depository services, there is an increased scope for market exploration as the market is turning even more heterogeneous by the day. Me and my partner here present before you a strategic approach for tapping this emerging market potential."

Rashv went on playing slides after slides of comparative charts, passionately charting out the strategic and marketing approach towards capturing the market as Priya looked on, highly impressed by the sharpness of his business mind.

The meeting went on for the entire day. The un-audited figures of the company were presented, the financial performance since the past three years, the future trend and the inter-company SWOT analysis was discussed threadbare. Several strategies were brainstormed and several conclusions were drawn and at the end, it was regarded as one of the most successful annual general meetings of the board in the past ten years of the company. The conference closed and congratulatory messages started beeping on Rashv's Blackberry. The success of the meeting bode well for his professional progress.

It was nothing but the pinch of losing his love that drove Rashv so deep into his profession. It was also partly responsible for his sudden meteoric rise. The distraction that the job at one of the busiest stock broking firms in the country offered and the long hours at work ironically made life and its burdens a bit more bearable for him with nowhere to go, nothing else but work to keep his mind occupied and no memory lanes to slip down to. He even lost touch with the most well-meaning of his friends. At night his tired body and mind gave no way to his wandering thoughts as sleep descended easily upon his work-weary eyes as soon as he hit the sack.

A week after the presentation, Rashv was working late into the evening when his phone beeped with a message. It was a message from Priya on Whatsapp. She and friends had planned for a night out at Chillout Zone, their favourite hanging out place.

"Heyy Rashv! Come on now. Come out of that life sucking cabin! Let's party tonight! Enough goals achieved for the week." Rashv was reluctant to come out of the office as he did not want any distractions of daily life to refresh the memories he was trying his best to evade. Even though the number had been an obsession for him in the past, a kneejerk reaction to take control of his fate in his own hands, he decided that now it was time to take a final shot at his destiny and look for the 23rd girl.

As it turned out, in time Rashv slowly came out his self-imposed shell of sorrow and tears and finally started mixing with people, if only to test his theory. As he started coming out for social meetings, the pain from the past hurts started to fade bit by bit. The cortisol flowing in his veins was being replaced by the adrenaline of pursuit. He had set his eyes on meeting the 23 rd girl of his life. Far from being a rebound relationship, he thought, this could prove to be the most meaningful relationship of his life. The realisation that it was also the 23rd year of his life blinded his pursuit even more. Something definitive was going to happen and very soon! So he jumped headlong into the dating pool, crossed his heart and hoped to make it this time around and ace his own number game.

As it turned out, at one of the office parties, he was randomly introduced to Ahana, a beautiful friend of Priya's. She was a fashion photographer and it was evident that she had a thing for beauty as she herself was full of beauty and poise. Her red lips were a perfect contrast to her honey brown skin and big bold eyes, captivating in their charm. The curvilinear waist and the saffron glow on her face made it almost impossible for Rashv to look away from her, even once. He felt a fierce attraction to her personality which was almost primitive in its quality and need. It had been a long time since butterflies had raided his entire nervous system and afflicted it with such a raw attraction. It was a very strong pull and it felt like it was meant to be that way. It was meant to be, his mind constantly analysed. The 23rd one he met had to be special! They instantly hit it off with each other. She too seemed to admire his razor sharp looks and he fell for her doe-eyed beauty. They chatted till the party got over.

KNOCK KNOCK!

Mind calling Heart! Mind calling Heart!

"She is the one! She has to be the one. The girl you have been waiting for. This is the 23rd girl", the mind gasped in sheer excitement. "Moreover, above anything else, the feelings are all hitting me so hard this time!"

The heart was weary of the mind ruling over Rashv for so

long and was not to be heard. It was tired of the number game and heartbreaks including the recent one with Roohi and was still covered in bandages from the impact.

"I do not know anything about all that anymore", it replied as the mind jumped. "This is it! We are here."

Chapter 27

"What's up!" he got a message on his BBM early in the morning.

"Ah! 8.23 am. That's a good sign!" he smiled.

"Nothing, just lying wide awake. Lost in your thoughts, Madame", he put his heart directly on the line.

"My Gosh. The most eligible bachelor around here was busy with my thoughts!" she replied with a winking smiley.

They kept on chatting till late in the morning. Rashv was over the moon for finally having met the right one even though he thought that it was too early for him to confess to her that he had actually begun to think of her as a perpetual love interest.

Days went by and life went on smoothly for him. Everything was going on as expected.

One night he was resting in bed after a particularly tiring day and he wondered, "Gut instincts about many things in life are actually true. Even though this number game began as an ego thing for me and it all actually sounds crazy and totally unthinkable, now that I look back and think of all that I have been up to with so many girls, can it be true that she is indeed the one for me, only because she is the 23rd one I have met! But after all, life is about taking chances. If you don't attempt something, you can never know whether it's right or wrong for you."

Could any of the other girls have been the right one for him? If something like that could be true, he may have already walked out on his true love, long back! If not, it had been nothing less than a cruel journey for everyone involved in it. Even though he now cringed at his teenage theory and somehow having followed it mindlessly till now, he smiled that incorrect or not, focusing on the number had indeed got him to make some life altering changes with his self. Amidst all these thoughts was also the realization that even though he had started thinking of spending his life with her and finally end the number game with the 'right girl' on a happy note as she seemed to like him too, he had not spilled the beans as yet. He felt that it was proper to admit to her the importance she had in his life, that he wanted to spend his life with her and as to why she was the right one for him. He decided to make it all clear to her without any delay.

It was the weekend and they met at the local bar with a group of friends to celebrate their friend Jess' birthday. Rashv was very nervous as he had decided to bare his heart to Ahana. Every one of their friends was there. Probably that gave him more of a cold feet syndrome than anything else. They were kicking back, laughing and giggling at some bad karaoke singers and having plain fun. Everyone was in their lightest element.

And then suddenly an announcement was heard, "Next on stage, Rashv Patel!"

He noticed that his best friend Rahul had gone ahead and suggested his name for the next performance. Rashv knew all too well that singing was not his cup of tea and he did not want to be made fun of in such a setting.

"Rahul you are gonna have it from me", he jeered.

But even as he feared of what people may think of his singing skills, he decided to take the situation and turn it around as a beautiful idea struck his mind.

He took the mike and began to belt out, the lyrics of one of the sweetest love songs ever. Brian Adams. Everything I do.

Look into my eyes, you will see,

What you mean to me.

... Don't tell me, it's not worth tryin' for,

The 23rd Girl

You can't tell me, it's not worth dyin' for…

You know, it's true,

Everything I do, I do it for you!

He smiled as he managed to sing as well as he could, possibly; all the time keeping his gaze on Ahana. It was kind of very evident to everyone at the bar that it was for her. As he finished his singing and bowed before the cheering crowd, he saw Ahana turn red, pick up her stuff and run away.

"My God! Was she blushing! Maybe I shouldn't have made it all so public", he thought.

That night, after that open declaration of affection, he did not even have the courage to text her. It was the most nervous he had felt in quite some time, nervous to know how she felt for him, nervous to know her reaction. He kept on dialing her number and cancelling the call till eventually, he gathered enough courage to actually wait for her to take the call.

"Hullo!"

"Hi! This is Rashv. Uhh…"

"Hi Rashv, I myself have been thinking of calling you!" she replied. "I was thinking about you and what happened today. What has been going on here?" she said.

"Ahh, I… dedicated that song to you on karaoke today. I wanted to talk to you about it."

She took a deep breath, gained control over her irregular breathing and continued, "When I heard that song and realised that you dedicated it to me, I felt like telling you what had been on my heart and mind for the longest time since I met you. You are truly special for me and I have not met anyone close to what you are... smart, funny, intelligent and truly attractive. In fact, you are the sweetest, funniest and the friendliest person I have known, a complete package, right from a dream sequence. I cannot tell you how happy I am, just to have met you. But Rashv, I have to tell you this: I want to keep our relationship to a sweet bond, perhaps... if you may like it that way. And I would like to continue to know you as a great guy, a good friend and beautiful company, beyond anything else", she paused and took another deep breath, probably sensing if she was ready to say what she was going to. "I am sorry Rashv I cannot love you in the way you love me. I don't really have the time to get into an emotional connection with a man at this point in my life when I myself am sorting out in my head about what I really want from life. I hope you understand. We have flirted, that's certain... but I .. I did not know that you had other thoughts. This is not what I want and I am telling you this from the deepest recesses of my heart. But we could always be friends and I would always be there for you."

"Are you sure?" Rashv asked, shell-shocked as he felt his heart feel too heavy to stay in the right place. He felt giddy and out of focus.

"Yes I am... and I'm really very sorry for all what has happened", she replied and cancelled the call.

"This cannot be. This simply cannot be," he shrieked in shock. "Wasn't she supposed to be the one? Didn't she have to be the one for me? Wasn't she Girl number 23!? Is this some kind of a mistake?" He screamed.

It felt like it was the end of the world. All his adolescent theories came crashing down like a pack of cards. The situation failed to make sense to him. "How did I not know? What is all this mess all about!" he shrieked. Rashv's heart was shattered in many pieces, for the 23rd time, so to say. As he kept the phone down, he thought of the million ways in which the number had backfired upon him and how he had still followed it nonetheless. He was so blind! In the end, he had even lost the stupid bet. The bet he played against fate, for the sake of his own life and love. Everything felt hollow and meaningless. His heart limped as all his assumptions had come to a dead end. In the end, it had all amounted to nothing, just as he had feared at times when he thought of breaking the pledge. What good had all this come to? Nothing! Had he simply wasted his time? The make-believe world he had been living in seemed to be a great deal easier than the sharpness of the real world whose reality now hit him like a splinter and bled him more than any physical hurt ever could.

"Can anyone please tell me what am I supposed to do now? I feel like a total loser!" He winced as he crossed his arms over his chest and closed his eyes. Tears trickled down his cheeks down to the pillow, staining it for the n-th time. He tried hard to understand as to why the number had not worked for him as it used to and whenever it mattered the most to him. As he recalled each and every token of love he had ever received from any possible girl in his life, he reached the same conclusion every time. The number had finally and definitely failed him. He got up from the bed and decided to throw away the meaningless souvenirs he had collected over the years that adorned his 'Shelf of Broken Hearts' and shove them into the dustbin or maybe destroy them, forever... those painful reminders of a lost deal and lost time. He looked at them for the final time as he began moving them to the bin... 1st... 2nd... 3rd... 4th... 5th... 6th... 7th... 10th... 15th... 20th... 21st... 22nd... 23rd...

"Wait, what... what... what... what!!! This 23rd one is from... Roohi??? Whattt??? It's from Roohi??? Howwwwwwww???" He screeched as he looked at a half dried rose wilted in his forgotten love, eyes wide with shock and disbelief. "There has been a mistake! How can this be! It cannot be!" he was delirious.

He went over the entire stuff and counted again twice, thrice, ten times!

THE 23RD GIRL

"What?? How on Earth has this happened! I have never been so stupid in my whole life!!!" he squealed. He went over the souvenirs and recalled a hot afternoon almost 6 years back when he had decided to sort and place these souvenirs from his childhood onto the shelf. He had missed Aarna's hand-drawn card! She had been his friend in middle school. He laughed at the sudden memory. It was done with an unstable hand, scribbled in yellow with his name written below it. He smiled and cried.

"But I have lost you Roohi! I have lost you forever!" he shrieked. "How could I not know? I had never loved so much, so hard and so true, ever before. I have been such a big fool. I have let go of you myself. I am the criminal of my own life! What do I do now?!" he screamed. The old wounds had begun to start oozing out again. It was a dark night of hopeless realisations for Rashv. He had answered his own questions. He was not puzzled anymore. He just lay in his bed as he recalled his past self and wondered as to how he could be as stupid as he had been.

EPILOGUE

"Yet each man kills the thing he loves
By each (of you) let this be heard
Some do it with a bitter look
Some with a flattering word
The coward does it with a kiss
The brave man with a sword"

— Oscar Wilde,

The Ballad Of Reading Gaol

Rashv read the Facebook update by one of his friends and tears rolled out of his eyes. He visualized himself as the cowardly backstabber who had betrayed Roohi and in utter frustration; he banged his hand hard on the table. He was about to push himself up to get some fresh breath of air by standing in his veranda when a notification popped up on his computer screen.

He immediately made a phone call and spoke incessantly, his tone that of guilt and pleading to meet. He hung up after deciding the time and venue for the meet.

Rashv simply couldn't believe what had just happened. He thanked his stars and Mr. Zuckerberg in particular. He waited for the day to end in the expectation that his stars would shine a tad brighter the next morning.

"Dude, I know you would not notice me when there is a beauty sitting in front of you. But still..."

Rashv woke up and acknowledged his presence as they hugged each other patting their back in a mock slap.

"God! Look at you! You have changed completely and this is simply unbelievable. I had never thought that you two will come together. My childhood buddy and my classmate in school who used to hate me like anything", beamed Rashv as he hugged and welcomed Rahul's friend.

"And you too! From fat to Oh my... my... what shall I say? Pepperoni Hot!"

"Life is a game of snake and ladders. You may get the chance to climb the highest ladder and come down the table just as easily when the snake of ill luck bites!" Rashv reflected as they settled across the table.

"Goodness! Such philosophy! Anyway, you just disappeared after our graduation. Good to see you after such a long time", she beamed.

"Well, that's a long story, more on that later. I have some pressing issues to handle before things get out of control", Rashv said as he sat looking a bit relieved. He narrated the whole story of his breakups and life so far to Aarna and Rahul and also about Roohi and how he had always felt like she was the one and about how he had hurt her. He felt relieved as he unburdened his heart to them. They listened patiently. Rahul suggested him to reach Dubai immediately and make amends as he slipped a note across to Rashv, with details of Roohi's current address. Roohi had left Mumbai with details of her correspondence to Rahul just in case Rashv changed his mind and would have liked to contact her. She got in touch with Rahul over social networking when Rashv decided to begin ignoring her. Rashv felt bouts of nervous tension as he held the small piece of paper in his sweaty palms and felt the weight of his emotions roll down from the corners of his eyelids. Rahul assured him that if Roohi was the one true love of his life she would forgive him if at all he truly meant what he said.

Rashv decided to switch shores and reach Dubai and meet the love of his life, as soon as possible. They bought an air ticket to Dubai and he took off the very next morning.

~~~~~~~~

Rashv's guilty heart was desperate to have one glance of the apple of his eye, his Roohi and woo her back. He knew that it would be an uphill task but he was pretty confident that he would win her back despite all odds and he flew to Dubai with hope and love in his heart.

This is the reason why you should always listen to your heart. They are like a non-complicated GPS. Hearts see a single road when minds see two.

Rashv had myriad thoughts on his mind as the flight carried on. He had never felt as nervous in his entire lifetime. He was risking breaking his heart once again but that was the thing. There was nothing more important in the world in that instant than his love for Roohi.

His mind was caught in feelings of fear and doubt. It called him stupid for taking on the risk of rejection. This was a rejection, which would break him beyond his thoughts. It told him that he risked being called foolish and selfish. It called him selfish for how he had surrendered to his whims and number games when it came to Love. He was apprehensive of how in the world he would face her; what all Roohi might say; about whether she still had the same feelings for him as before? Would she forgive him? Had she moved on? He was full of guilt for having hurt her in the way he did. For having assigned her a number and reduced her importance in his life. He thought: But if ever I had not surrendered to this game of fate, would I ever have met her? His mind was a mixed bag of thoughts: fear, guilt and love.

KNOCK KNOCK!

It was Heart calling the Mind.

> "Leave everything behind
> Stomp on the road of your dreams,
> Trust the voice of your heartbeats,
> As life meets you midway in your tryst"

For the first time in his life, his heart had found its courageous voice. He smiled and let his heart convince him as he closed his eyes and let a swarm of memories descend upon his eyelids.

His reverie was broken with the announcement that the flight had finally landed. It felt like three hundred thousand hours of a long journey had ended.

As soon as he reached the airport, he made the first frantic call to Roohi and after that several other which went unattended. His heart sunk as he thought that Roohi had decided against meeting him. Tears rolled down his cheeks as he prayed for a single chance to meet the true love of his life and apologise. He felt shattered at the thought that Roohi was not taking any calls from him. Dejected, he sat in the waiting arena with his eyes closed, all his hopes and dreams wearing thin. He wasn't able to contact her. Should he go straight to her house? What if she refused to talk to him? What if she slammed the door on his helpless face? He was feeling nervous and heartbroken. He stared at the piece of paper with Roohi's address on it as he decided against his doubts and took the decision to walk up to her door and ask for her forgiveness.

"My poor girl! What all must I have made her go through in my silly whimsical pursuits!" He picked his backpack and made his way out of the airport.

~~~~~~~~~

Roohi cut the stems of the beautiful big roses growing outside her window and assorted them in a broken vase. In this big bad world, nothing is perfect. Neither one's dreams, nor one's reality. With time, she had learned to appreciate the brokenness of things. A broken heart, a broken dream, a broken piece of her favourite miniature art attained new meanings and became pieces of history to her, each carrying a story of having changed and evolved and been made real enough to fit in the imperfect reality of life. And no longer in the whole wide world had she enough courage to pick up the fallen pieces, throw them as waste and replace them with something new, for she herself was broken too and she could not bargain the shards of her broken heart for the love of someone else. In her brokenness, Roohi felt close to Rashv. She found herself near his thoughts all the time. For in the world of lovers, pain and pleasure are inseparable. It was the precise reason why she had not allowed herself to get over the memories of Rashv. She did not simply want to get over. It had become a blue-grey world as life was constantly playing on the rewind in her mind instead of taking her forward. Or maybe she herself loved the four steps backward, two steps forward dance that kept her in her old meaningful past.

Fallen flowers smell just as sweet, she reminded herself as she smiled and picked up a rose from the ground, adorning it in her thick hair.

The mellifluous voice of Taylor Swift wafted softly in the vacant spaces of her small lonely apartment, filling it with tender notes of love.

> "Missing him was dark grey, all alone,
> Forgetting him was like trying to know,
> Someone you have never met,
> But loving him was Red,
> Loving him was Red."

She smiled. Taylor Swift was the modern Goddess of Love, it seemed. She knew and sang of almost all the undertones of love one could ever feel. It had been six months since they had last spoken to each other and more than a physical separation, it was a painful uncoupling of his heart from hers. For days altogether she had wilted in the withdrawal symptoms he had unleashed upon her poor soul. For months she had writhed in insufferable pain. It had felt like losing a limb, the breaking of her heart; she remembered. Since then, her heart was constantly aching and missing, constantly bleeding. As she tied the red roses in a neat ribbon, she wondered how entangled she herself felt. Still full of love, still full of hopes and dreams of "one day, he will..."

She took a deep breath and muttered, "You seem to have taken away my memory with you. The only thing I remember is you, Rashv. Why did you have to wreck my life like this, my Love! Where have you gone, taking everything I ever had, along with you?" she asked.

Suddenly her heart became so heavy that she sank into her sofa, staring blankly at the white ceiling.

"Life has quietened so badly. It has been months ever since I had my last job", she thought. She sighed and wondered whether the cobwebs of her memories would let her live.

Her attention was diverted by the loud ringing of the doorbell.

"Who can it be?" she reluctantly got up from the chair. It was Rashv. She double checked. It was Rashv indeed.

For a second she was taken aback. It was a whole lot of mixed feelings she had within that short span of time when her eyes met his... surprise, disbelief, joy, sadness and pain. "There's a lot more to life than saying the right things at the right time, Rashv!"

Rashv felt his tender feelings quickly convert into despair as he caught a hint of resentment in her tone and his hopes crashed to the floor.

"You have every right in the world to hate me Roohi! But can you please give me one last chance to say something?"

"Of course!" she looked into Rashv's eyes and saw how desperate he looked as she searched for meaning in those eyes that were now turning moist. She wanted to know what really was hidden in the bottom of his heart. She wanted to believe him once again even though it felt like one of the most difficult things she had ever done. For ever since Rashv made an unexplained exit from her life, she had built walls around her foolish heart for people. Walls, that if they tried to climb, they'd hurt themselves before hurting her.

With Rashv, Roohi had allowed herself a freefall for the first time in Life. It had felt so right and so true with him that it actually felt like she was being lifted into something serene and beautiful whenever they were together. It felt weird to have this connection. It was unnatural to be at so much ease. Every time they were together, she felt like she was falling into a dizzy spiral like it was an irrecoverable condition. But now it was different. Six months of unexpected separation hurt. The unsaid goodbyes hurt even more. She had struggled to assign meaning to days. Even leaving for another country did not help as his beautiful smile was like a negative imprint on her mind. Wherever she looked, she saw him. And now when Rashv was here, she found herself struggling between wanting to see him once again, not wanting to see him, ask him all the 'Whys' that he had preferred not to answer and probably fight with him for creating a mess out of her dreams but she was not sure whether she still owned him like before. She felt all her questions resurface and go numb. She was hurt. Did the past matter as much anymore? She did not want to be hurt again.

It was ten minutes of awkward silence between them as Roohi finally took a deep breath and smiled gently.

"Come in", she said.

Rashv nodded and followed her like a guilty kid.

They sat across each other in a numb silence as if mourning for a shared past. Sometimes a quiet company for the grieving heart soothes a lot more than actual words.

Rashv broke the silence as he saw a tear form on Roohi's

eyelids that she was quick to hide. She was looking aside. Probably it was because that the weight of the past memories attached with this person sitting across was so much that she feared she would break down if she looked at him for too long.

"I know I have done you a world of wrong Roohi. I feel really guilty sitting here in front of you with my mind full of so many emotions and not able to start anywhere."

"You know what? You don't need to apologise to me Rashv. I have often thought of the day when I first caught a glimpse of you and fell head over heels. It took me just one day to fall in love with you Rashv. And it took just one day for you to forget me. What, when and why were the only questions that you left me with as a parting gift. All the moments we had, the spark I thought we had, did it mean nothing? Could it all be forgotten in a day? Was it so superficial? Maybe for you, it was. You broke my heart and I waited for you. But all I had was silence. And I took that as your answer." Roohi sounded heartbroken. Her throat was choked with tears at the memory of what all Rashv had made her endure in so many days.

For a moment, again the air around them was thick and heavy with emotion. Rashv did not know what to say. He had brought immense pain to the girl who loved him so much and to his own heart by looking for the girl of his dreams when she was right there, waiting to be gathered up and loved like never before and never again. He felt jabs of pain in his heart.

"Roohi, I know I have been the most foolish person alive or maybe more than that. I have hurt you beyond my thoughts. I am sorry I was scared of committing so much so soon but believe me, there has been nobody who has been or can be or ever will be, more important than what you are to me. It was true and always will be, there's been only one person whom I have always felt free to be myself with and that is you."

THE 23RD GIRL

She was silent, her lashes wet with tears. In those moments, she felt all the love she had for Rashv rise up to the surface, even as the memory of how much she had been through and how long she bore separation from him choked her throat.

Rashv continued in a low voice, heavy with emotion, "I have been selfish and maybe that was because I have been foolishly protective of my silly heart which has been broken so many times. It's true that I got scared. It's true that I ran away. But it's also true that in all these days, in the countless hours that each day held, the only person I constantly thought about was you, Roohi. Life has been tough for me ever since I let go of you. Sometimes I even thought I deserved all this pain, after having hurt you in the way that I did, but my heart was bursting with so much pain that it felt like it would be better to die of love than of longing and that is why I could not stay away anymore. I am yours, Roohi, take me or leave me." He took a step towards her, with all the urgency he felt, and they stood close, face-to-face. Then he reached for her hand and curved his fingers around hers. She looked at that clasp, his hand warm and callused like before, his touch making her shiver, just like before. And even though she had been hurt and there had been pain and half-trust, it seemed like nothing at all had changed when he touched her, probably except for the time and their circumstances. She felt her insides melt with an old love. Their eyes were steady and their gaze was unflickering and in between the free-flowing tears that both of them did not struggle to stop, they shared every single emotion they felt, in their shared silence tempered by their quickening heartbeats: true and tender. Rashv stepped up and kissed her velvet lips. With that kiss, Rashv had brought them both back to life. It felt like life had entered her lifeless body yet again, after so many days of living on a half-breath. "Marry me", he said. "Please marry me, Roohi. Marry me and be called Roohi Patel. Or keep your sweet name, but whatever you wish to call yourself, please be mine and never leave me, for I cannot bear another day of my life to go by that does not have you in it", he pleaded.

"And don't you ever do this to me again!" she said, half tears, half smiles. It was like a new birth, a reincarnation of old love, a flare up of an old flame and kindling of new hopes. Finally, there would be a beginning of the happily-ever-after for them too.

ABOUT THE AUTHORS:

DIVYA believes that every person is a live story and that everyone we meet and every experience we have forms a part of that story. When she is not sieving through her experiences to collect her stories, she is a doting mommy to a tiny dictator along with managing a career with the country's largest public sector bank. She has been an active blogger with the Half Baked Beans' blog Half Baked Voices along with a family of ten other bloggers. This is her first book.

ROHAN KACHALIA is an avid reader and writer whose love for writing kicked in when he started blogging 5 years ago. Since then, he has penned many fictional stories and poems. His short stories and poems have been published in various anthologies. The 23rd Girl is his first co-authored novel.

You can get in touch with him on at: Twitter- @rohank01

If you're a movie buff or love watching television shows, you can buy merchandise of your favourite movie/TV series at a discounted price NOW.

Just log on to **greenrockstore.com** and use the coupon code '**ROCK20**' to avail **discount** up to **20%**.

Other Titles by Half Baked Beans
Available on Amazon and Flipkart

Heartbreak In Progress
...proceed with caution
RITIKA | CHITRA

Love, Again

Edited by Rethra.A

NIKHIL UPRETY
THE MAUT-E-MATICIANS

AN EYE FOR AN EYE
ASHUTOSH GARG

COALESCENCE
Shivam Singh

REAL ILLUSION
MAHI GOYAL

YAMA
Kevin Missal

All I Need is YOU
MUKUND VERMA

KALIYUG
The Secret Plot
B.S.Sarwagna Kumar

NO TIME TO PAUSE

Pavithra Ramesh

SCARLET NIGHTS

MAYUR PATEL

tagged

M Kaarthika Santhosh

WILD CARD

Asfiya Rahman

THE INDIAN AMERICAN DREAM

PRANAY SAHU

Thank You Love...

"Taking love beyond words"

Ayush Gupta

The Fence

Stories from HBB Workshop

Curtain

Compiled and Edited by
Rafaa Dalvi

BLEMISHING THE ODDS

Harish Penumarthi